COLD
CASE
MURDER

SHIRLEE MCCOY

D0017874

Steeple
Hill®

Published by Steeple Hill Books™

Special thanks and acknowledgment to Shirlee McCoy for her contribution to the Without a Trace miniseries.

STEEPLE HILL BOOKS

Steeple
Hill®

Recycling programs
for this product may
not exist in your area.

ISBN-13: 978-0-373-44330-7
ISBN-10:   0-373-44330-7

COLD CASE MURDER

www.SteepleHill.com

Printed in U.S.A.

"Jodie?"

Harrison spoke quietly, but there was a steel edge to his voice, and she turned to face him again, her breath catching as she met his eyes. Eyes that looked deep into hers and seemed to see all the secrets she tried hard to keep hidden. The insecurity. The fear. The feeling she'd gotten on the wrong path.

"Yeah?" she asked.

"Whatever you know, whatever you're hiding, you're going to have to tell me eventually."

"Maybe, but not today." Not a lie, but not quite the truth either. Telling Harrison would mean admitting that she was scared. More scared than she'd been in a long time.

Harrison stared her down for a moment, his eyes searching her face. "Fair enough, but you may as well know that there are very few secrets the dead can hide from me. I'm not too shabby about getting the truth from the living either. If what's bothering you has something to do with this case, you won't be able to keep it from me for long."

* * *

WITHOUT A TRACE: Will a young mother's disappearance bring a bayou town together...or tear it apart?

Books by Shirlee McCoy

Love Inspired Suspense

Die Before Nightfall
Even in the Darkness
When Silence Falls
Little Girl Lost
Valley of Shadows
Stranger in the Shadows
Missing Persons
Lakeview Protector
*The Guardian's Mission
*The Protector's Promise
Cold Case Murder

*The Sinclair Brothers

Steeple Hill Single Title

Still Waters

SHIRLEE MCCOY

has always loved making up stories. As a child, she daydreamed elaborate tales in which she was the heroine—gutsy, strong and invincible. Though she soon grew out of her superhero fantasies, her love for storytelling never diminished. She knew early that she wanted to write inspirational fiction, and began writing her first novel when she was a teenager. Still, it wasn't until her third son was born that she truly began pursuing her dream of being published. Three years later she sold her first book. Now a busy mother of four, Shirlee is a homeschool mom by day and an inspirational author by night. She and her husband and children live in Washington State and share their house with a dog and a guinea pig. You can visit her Web site at www.shirleemccoy.com.

It is for freedom that Christ has set us free.
Stand firm, then, and do not let yourselves
be burdened again by a yoke of slavery.
—*Galatians* 5:1

PROLOGUE

New Orleans, Louisiana
FBI Headquarters, Missing Persons Unit

At night, if she dreamed at all, Jodie Gilmore dreamed of Loomis, Louisiana—the thick, ugly scent of the swamp in summer heat, the shadowy gloom of stately manor homes gone to ruin, the tension that shrouded the little town. There were secrets there. And demons. Not the made-up kind. The real-life, haunt-you-forever kind. The kind that came from loss and heartache and loneliness. It didn't matter that she'd left town the day she'd turned eighteen or that ten years had passed since then, Jodie still shuddered every time she thought of the place. The day she had gotten into her beat-up Mustang and headed for wherever the road would take her, she promised she'd never return.

It seemed she was about to break that promise.

"Well? What are your thoughts?" Miles Jordan's voice held a note of impatience, and Jodie scanned the contents of the missing person's file for the second time since she'd walked into her supervisor's office, hoping that this time the words would stick.

Leah Farley. Twenty-eight. Widowed mother of a three-year-old girl. Went missing two weeks after her husband was found dead. Last seen in Loomis, Louisiana.

Jodie set the file down and met her supervisor's emotionless gray eyes. "It looks pretty straightforward. The woman killed her husband, tried to make it look like a suicide and ran when the investigation revealed the truth."

"Don't be so quick to jump to conclusions, Agent Gilmore. As the file indicates, Leah Farley's shoe was found on the grounds of a house out by the swamplands near a boarded-up tunnel on the porch of a house that once served as part of the Underground Railroad. There was blood on it."

Jodie didn't ask what house. She didn't need to. She knew. Just as she knew every nook and cranny of the town she'd grown up in. What she didn't know was why her mother had run from it twenty-five years ago. "The blood is probably her husband's."

"Like I said, let's not jump to conclusions." Miles steepled his fingers beneath his chin and eyed her from across the table. "There's been a lot going on in Loomis. A couple of murders, an attempted kidnapping. The local PD is investigating, and we're working in conjunction with them, assuming the incidents aren't simply a succession of unrelated crimes."

"Sam Pierce is the lead on this?"

"Right. He's feeling like the locals would be more comfortable with someone they know. Maybe with you there, they'll open up and talk a little more."

"People in Loomis don't talk. Not even to each other." The words escaped, and Miles's lips tightened into a hard line.

"Agent Gilmore, your assignment is to work as liaison between our team and the people of Loomis. Do you have a problem with that?"

"Of course not, sir." Only six months into her FBI career and still on probation, Jodie couldn't afford to get a reputation for balking at assignments. Not when she'd worked so hard to get where she was.

"Good. Go home. Pack your things and head out."

"Now?" That was a million years too soon.

"Yes. Good luck, agent." His curt nod was a dismissal Jodie couldn't ignore, and she stepped blindly out the office door. The die had been cast. The decision made. There was absolutely nothing she could do about it. She was going back to Loomis whether she liked it or not.

And she didn't like it.

She didn't like it at all.

ONE

Even with the windows of her car rolled up, Jodie could smell the bayou. Heavy moist air with a bite of decay to it. Not as bad as it got in the heat of the summer but bad enough to make her nose wrinkle. Or maybe it was disgust that was doing that. There were plenty of places she'd imagined the FBI might send her, but back to Loomis wasn't one of them. Here she was, returning to the one place she'd been determined never to visit again.

She turned onto a narrow dirt driveway that wound uphill and away from the bayou, braking lightly as she neared a neglected farmhouse that stood in the center of an overgrown clearing near the swamp. Abandoned decades ago, it had been vacant for more years than Jodie had been alive. A tunnel dug beneath the house led to a room that had once served as a stop on the Underground Railroad. Later it had served other, less altruistic purposes—as a storage place for moonshine during prohibition, a drug den for hippies in the sixties. Eventually, the town council voted to have the tunnel and the house boarded up.

What the missing woman, Leah Farley, had been doing there, Jodie didn't know. She planned to find out, though. And quickly. The sooner she helped Sam Pierce solve the case, the sooner she could wipe the Loomis dirt off her feet and get back to her life.

Rain drizzled from the sky as Jodie climbed out of her car and started across the yard. Despite her misgivings about being back in Loomis, anticipation hummed through her. Working for the FBI had been her dream for as long as she could remember. Solving cases, putting bad guys behind bars, was what she was meant to do. Even if she had to do it in Loomis.

"Agent Gilmore, glad you could make it to the party." A tall, dark-haired man she recognized stepped out onto the porch, and Jodie smiled a greeting as she picked her way up dry-rotted porch stairs.

"It's good to be included, Agent Pierce."

"How about I call you Jodie and you call me Sam? It'll make things easier." He smiled, and Jodie could see why so many women in the New Orleans office had set their sights on the handsome agent. Recently, rumors had been circulating that he'd gotten engaged to a child psychologist in Loomis. True or not, it wasn't any of Jodie's concern. She didn't waste time on men and relationships. Not anymore.

"Whatever you say, Sam. Did you find anything in the house?"

"We did."

"Leah Farley?"

"No. And no evidence that she's been inside."

"So what did you find?" Curious, Jodie followed Sam into the musty foyer, her mind racing with possibilities. Ransom note. Clothing. Forensic evidence. Any of those could help bring the case to a successful end.

"We found two bodies."

"*Two* bodies?" She glanced around the dust-covered foyer, half expecting to see the remains lying nearby.

"Skeletons, to be more accurate. They're in a hidden room

down in the basement. They've been there for a while. Decades probably."

"Did they have identification?"

"Not that we could see, but the sheriff agreed not to let anyone touch the remains yet. I've got a man coming in from New Orleans to do that. A forensic anthropologist."

"When will he get here?"

"Shouldn't be long. I called him an hour ago."

"Do you mind if I take a look at the scene while we wait?" Now that she was in Loomis, Jodie wanted out of it. Waiting for someone to come along and help make that happen didn't work for her.

"Sure. It's this way."

Half-rotted boards creaked beneath her feet as Jodie followed Sam into the basement. The sound shivered along her spine, reminding her of all the stories she'd heard about the house when she was a kid, stories about spooks and haunts and things that went bump in the night. Jodie had always known them for what they were—a perfect way to keep kids from exploring a house that might not be structurally sound. Still, she had to admit the place was creepy, its shadowy corners concealing more than they revealed.

"Careful on these stairs, Jodie. Some of them are completely rotted through." Sam led her into a basement lit by electric torches and gestured to a hole in the far wall. "There's the tunnel. There were boards covering it, but it looked like they'd been taken down and replaced quickly. We've already got them tagged as evidence."

Several uniformed officers were standing in the room, none of them familiar to Jodie. She had to admit she was relieved. Eventually she'd have to face people from her past, but she'd rather it be later than sooner.

She crossed the room and surveyed the opening. Five feet

high. Maybe three feet wide. "It would be a tight squeeze for someone carrying a body."

"But not so tight it would be impossible. Especially not if the body was being dragged. After so long, there isn't evidence to indicate that's what happened, but we can't say it didn't, either. Hopefully Cahill will shed some light on things."

"Cahill?"

"The forensic anthropologist I told you about. He'll re-create the scene based on what he finds, then work to identify our victims. Come on in, but watch your head." He stooped down and walked into the tunnel.

Jodie borrowed a flashlight one of the officers offered and followed. "*Our* victims? Isn't the case a local matter?"

"It should be, but since we were in here following up on the Leah Farley case, the sheriff asked if we'd be willing to help with victim identification. I agreed."

"Who's the sheriff around here now?" She hoped not the same one who'd been sheriff when Jodie was growing up.

"Bradford Reed."

Of course it was the same sheriff. Otherwise things, would have been a little too comfortable. "I remember him."

"Good. The Leah Farley case may be connected to the murders that have occurred in town. Getting along with the local PD is imperative."

Then you shouldn't have called me in to help.

Jodie didn't say what she was thinking. There was no way she wanted to explain her teenage years. The subtle rebellions that had, more often than not, gotten her in trouble.

The scent of damp earth filled her nose, and cool, moist air settled on her skin as she stepped into a cavernous room. Her flashlight beam bobbed across a dirt floor littered with years of debris. Cloth. Plastic. A few old bottles. Near the far wall, a pile of rotted clothes lay amidst the other rubble. Even without getting closer, Jodie could make out the subtle shapes of the bones beneath. Two skulls lay side by side in the dirt, smooth and dingy yellow.

She moved closer, doing her best to stay detached and unaffected as she surveyed the remains. Stale air, ripe with the remnant of something putrid and old, filled her lungs. She ignored it, crouching down to get a better look. A fleshless skull stared up at her, its empty eye sockets and grinning teeth a macabre reminder of the life that had once been. The other skull was facedown, a two-centimeter sliver of bone missing from the base. Closer to the top of the skull, the bone was cracked.

"It would take a lot of force to crack a skull like that." She spoke the thought out loud, wanting to pick the skull up and examine it more closely but knowing she couldn't.

"A lot of force or a lot of rage."

"Any sign of the weapon?"

"Nothing. From the looks of the injury, we could be searching for anything. Baseball bat, butt of a gun, a club."

"Maybe something metal. A pipe?" Jodie responded by rote, her gaze riveted to a pile that lay beside the skulls. It looked as if a rodent had made a nest there, creating it from faded cloth and long strands of fine hair. Blond hair, from the looks of it. Even time and dirt couldn't quite hide the fact. More tufts of it were visible beneath the facedown skull. These were even easier to identify. Long. Straight.

White-blond?

If so, they were the same color as Jodie's. The same color her mother's had been. She shuddered, leaning in a little closer, trying to see more of what remained.

"You're getting a little close to the remains, ma'am. Maybe you should back up before you disturb something." The words were gruff and loud, and Jodie whirled toward the speaker, her flashlight illuminating a tall, dark-haired man who stood beside Sam.

"I'm not in the habit of disturbing crime scenes."

"Good to know." He strode across the room, his movements as lithe and graceful as a jungle cat's, his gaze so intense Jodie was tempted to look away.

"I take it you're the forensic anthropologist." She stood, careful not to step any closer to the skeletons.

"Harrison Cahill." His eyes were oddly light in a craggy face, his lips turned down in a scowl.

"Jodie Gilmore."

"I take it you're the agent working with Sam? And a fairly new one, right?" He said it almost absently as he moved up beside Jodie, his gaze moving from her to the mounds of cloth and bones.

"Does it matter?"

"I guess we'll find out." He met her eyes for a moment, then crouched down next to the skeletons, dismissing her with an abruptness that bordered on rude.

"Don't mind Cahill. He's like that with everyone." Sam moved in close, his voice filled with humor that spoke of familiarity.

"But more so with people who pull me away from big weekend plans," Harrison complained as he pulled out a digital camera and began taking pictures.

"Big weekend plans?"

"I've got six cases I'm working on for the New Orleans police."

"Then I'm doubly appreciative of your efforts here. Hopefully we can a get quick resolution." Sam crouched down next to Harrison, and the two men began discussing the remains. Male. Female. Early thirties.

Jodie watched silently, feeling useless. Completely unnecessary. Obviously not needed. The feeling was a bitter echo of the way she'd felt as a child when her father had pursued one woman after another and she'd been left alone, desperate to belong.

She shoved the feeling and the memories aside, refusing to acknowledge them. She was an accomplished professional, not an insecure kid. To prove it, she squatted down next to Sam, watching as Harrison snapped more pictures.

Harrison shot a look in her direction, his eyes telling her to back off.

She ignored him, focusing her attention on the dusty cloth that lay over the skeletons. A blanket of some kind? As the camera flashed, she saw other things. Bits of fabric printed with what might have been tiny flowers. A silver wedding band. The camera flashed again, and Jodie caught sight of something lying near the wall. Half-covered by dirt, the dull piece of metal could have been just about anything but looked like something very familiar.

She trained her light on it, squinting to get a better look. "Is that a bullet?"

Harrison shifted his attention from the scene he was documenting and looked in the direction the female agent's light was shining.

Jodie, she'd said her name was.

A young-sounding name for a very young-looking woman. Too young. Too inexperienced. Too much invading his space. He liked to take his time when he worked a scene, documenting it slowly, making sure he had a visual record of everything before anything was moved. He did not like people standing over his shoulder, distracting him from his methodical approach. "Looks like it. Now if we can find the weapon that fractured our victims' skulls, we'll have an even clearer idea of what went on here."

"And if we can't find the weapon?" The woman's voice was husky rather than sweet, and it didn't at all match her delicate looks.

"Then we'll figure out what happened other ways."

"What—"

"Look." He lowered his camera and met Jodie's eyes. "I

know you're new to the job and gung ho to know everything there is to know about everything, but I don't have the time or patience to explain my methods to you."

"I wasn't going to ask for an explanation of your methods, Mr. Cahill. I was going to ask what I could do to help." To her credit, she didn't sound defensive or offended by his blunt comment.

"Call me Harrison. And I appreciate the offer of help, but I prefer to work alone."

"This case is part of an ongoing investigation, so you'd better get used to having Jodie and me around. Mind if I grab that bullet?" Sam stepped toward the wall where the bullet lay, and Harrison was tempted to tell him that he did mind. He didn't want anything touched or moved until he was good and ready for it to be. And he wasn't ready.

Unfortunately, he wasn't the one calling the shots. The FBI was paying for him to be here. They'd want to have a say in how things were handled.

"Let me just snap a few more photos. Have you got a weapon you want to try and match it to?"

"No weapon, but we've got three other murder victims. Two were hit over the head and then shot."

"Recently?"

"Yeah."

"Then it isn't likely the cases are connected. These two have been here for a long time." Harrison took the photos and then stepped back, bumping into something warm, soft and most definitely female. He didn't have to turn around to picture Jodie—white-blond hair, heart-shaped face and wide, sad eyes.

"Sorry about that." He stepped quietly to the side, inhaling spring rain and summer flowers, his heart jumping in acknowledgment.

If Jodie heard his apology, she didn't acknowledge it or him. "What caliber is it, Sam?"

"Looks like a nine-millimeter."

"Does it match the caliber used to kill Dylan Renault and Earl Farley?"

"Yes, but a matching caliber doesn't mean a matching weapon." Sam placed the bullet in an evidence bag and moved toward the tunnel that led out of the room. "I'm going to take this out. See if I can get expedited ballistics testing on it. If the weapons are the same, we may be looking at the work of a serial killer."

"Seems like a long time between victims." Harrison leaned forward, gently lifting the blanket that covered the remains and folding it into an evidence bag.

"Yeah, it does. But maybe there are other victims we don't know about." Sam's words were grim, and he walked into the tunnel, his footsteps fading away.

Jodie remained in the room, and Harrison braced himself for the questions he was sure she'd ask. Instead of speaking, she watched silently. Harrison could feel her tension mounting as he began the process of cataloging and bagging one bone after another.

Was she upset by the bodies and caught up in imagining the victims' last moments? It happened sometimes, but not usually at scenes like this.

Finally, he couldn't ignore it any longer and turned from the tangle of long hair he was examining. "Are you okay?"

"Fine." But her voice trembled, and her hand shook as she brushed a thick strand of hair from her cheek. Blond hair. Similar to what Harrison was bagging. Was Jodie imagining herself lying dead on the ground, or was her reaction simply a case of rookie nerves? Seeing the dead was never an easy thing.

Pointing that out to Jodie wouldn't do any good. Harrison had worked with enough rookies to know that they'd rather pass out on the evidence than admit they were about to.

He carefully lifted a cervical vertebra, pausing when he caught sight of another bullet. "Do me a favor, will you? I've found a second bullet. Can you let Sam know?"

"Have you found the casings?" Whatever nerves she'd been feeling now seemed to have disappeared as she crouched beside him, her shoulder brushing his, the flowery scent he'd noticed earlier drifting around her.

"Not yet. That doesn't mean they're not here."

"I'll let Sam know." She stood and moved away, disappearing into the tunnel, her scent still lingering in the room.

The fact that he could still smell it as he bent back over the remains bothered Harrison more than he wanted to admit. It had been two years since Allison had thrown the engagement ring he'd given her across the room and stomped out of the house they'd planned to share after their wedding. One year and three months since she'd eloped with Jamison Bentley—a high-school teacher whose seven-to-four workdays and summers off were exactly what Allison had wanted from Harrison. It was the one thing Harrison hadn't been able to give her. His job was his passion, his calling. He had no plan to give it up.

Which was why he'd decided to avoid relationships, accept his life as a bachelor and be happy about it. It was also why he shouldn't be noticing Jodie's perfume. Or shampoo. Or whatever it was that clung to her skin.

Apparently, the past month had taken more of a toll on Harrison than he'd thought. Two weeks in California working with the FBI to identify remains left by a serial killer. Then back to New Orleans and twelve-hour days getting caught up on work. He needed a vacation. That was the problem.

It had to be, because there was no way Harrison planned to admit that he found a woman intriguing who looked like she was barely out of her teens.

With that firmly in mind, he turned his attention back to the man and woman lying on the ground in front of him. The nameless, faceless dead. He'd find out who they were and make sure their families had the closure they deserved. Nothing—not time, not scanty evidence, not a sweet-smelling distraction—would keep him from doing that.

TWO

Jodie stepped out of the house and into the damp March air, her heart beating in time to her pounding head. She never got headaches in New Orleans, but she'd had them plenty when she'd lived in Loomis. She should have known they'd be back as soon as she set foot in the little town.

Sam was a few yards away, talking to a uniformed officer, and Jodie walked toward them, determined to forget both the headache and the past. If she kept focused, kept moving forward on the case, there'd be no chance of sinking back into what she'd been a decade ago. "Sam? We've got another bullet in the tunnel. No casings yet, but Cahill isn't done collecting the evidence."

"Thanks for letting me know. I'll get it and send it with the other for ballistics testing, and—"

"You'll be wasting your time on that, Agent Pierce." The officer cut in, and Jodie took her first good look at him, her heart sinking when she realized who he was.

Sheriff Bradford Reed. His lined face and faded eyes sparked a memory of another day. Jodie had been cutting school, and he'd found her hanging out behind the library. He'd been neither cruel nor kind, his silent disapproval making Jodie feel worse than her father's rage had.

"Wasting my time because…?" Sam's question pulled

Jodie from the memory and she blinked, trying to free herself from the past.

"The crimes aren't related. We've got no mass murderer or serial killer or whatever name y'all want to put on it. This is a peaceful town—"

"A peaceful town where several murders have taken place, Sheriff Reed. I'm sure I don't need to remind you of the fact." Sam spoke with quiet conviction, and Jodie wondered if he and the sheriff had been on opposite sides of the fence during the course of the FBI's investigation into Leah Farley's disappearance.

"I know what's going on in my town. I'm just saying that what's happening now and what happened years ago aren't related. So there's no reason to waste time and money checking on those bullets. They're not going to match what we've already got."

"Maybe they're not, Sheriff, but it's our job to find out for sure." Jodie met the man's eyes and refused to fidget under his intense scrutiny. If she was lucky, he wouldn't recognize her.

Of course, she'd never been lucky.

"You're Jodie Gilmore."

"That's right."

"Been a long time."

"Ten years."

"Does your father know you're back in town?"

"Not yet."

"Guess you'll get around to telling him eventually." He shifted his attention back to Sam, dismissing her as he had when he'd dropped her off at her house so many years before. "Looks like we're done here. You'll let me know what your forensic specialist has to say about those bodies?"

"That and whether or not we get a match on the blood on Leah Farley's shoe."

"Good. See ya around, then." The sheriff nodded his head

in Jodie's direction, his eyes dull and lifeless. No motivation. No real need to find answers. If the murderer in his town was going to be found, Jodie had a feeling the sheriff was more than happy to leave the finding to the FBI.

"Sheriff Reed hasn't changed much." She spoke as the sheriff got into his car and drove away.

"He's always been unmotivated?"

"I'd call it indifferent, but I guess it means the same."

"What it means is that he'd be willing to let these people go unidentified. That's not acceptable to me."

"What about the other murders? Is he more motivated to solve them?" Jodie asked, though she was pretty sure she knew the answer.

"I think he was hoping for a cut-and-dried case, but the more answers we find, the more questions we have. I'm hoping that with you here, things will move along a little more quickly."

"You think I can get the answers you need?" His assumption was so far off base, she almost laughed. Not only would she not be able to get people in Loomis to talk, but also they might be more closedmouthed around her. She knew them, after all. Their pasts. Their secrets. Their vulnerabilities.

Just as they knew hers.

"You grew up here, Jodie. They're going to open up to a local in a way they won't open up to an outsider."

Maybe that was true, but in Loomis's eyes, she was an outsider. She didn't bother trying to explain. Only someone who had lived in the town could understand. "I'll do my best to be an asset to the investigation."

"I'm sure you will." His tone was serious, but Jodie could see amusement in his eyes.

She'd sounded like a rookie, and she suddenly felt like one. "Just so you know, this isn't my first case."

"Just so *you* know, that's why I called you in. You've got

great interrogation skills. Even if this hadn't been your home-town, I would have wanted you to step in. I'm going to get that bullet. Want to meet me at headquarters later? We can come up with a plan of action there."

"Headquarters?" The only headquarters she knew of was back in New Orleans, and she'd be perfectly happy to meet him there.

"We're renting a building on Main Street. It used to be a five-and-dime."

"I know it."

"You can go ahead and get settled in wherever you're going to stay before you head over there. I may be here awhile." He walked back to the house, and Jodie had no choice but to get in her car and drive away. The problem was, she didn't have anywhere to go. She'd already called Loomis Hotel, but all the rooms were booked.

Vera Peel's boardinghouse was creepy and old, the propri-etress stingy and mean, but it might work. Then there was Dad's. The family home. The place she should have been able to return to no questions asked. She couldn't. Even if she could have, she wouldn't. There was nothing for her in the colonial house she'd grown up in but unhappy memories and disappointments.

Which brought her right back to square one. Where would she stay while she was in Loomis?

Rain fell in steady rivulets as Jodie pulled down the long driveway. Twilight painted the landscape in shades of green and gold, making beauty of the bayou's murky water. In the distance, lights beckoned Jodie toward Loomis. If she hadn't known the truth about the town, she might have felt a tug of nostalgia as she passed old plantation homes covered with deep green ivy.

She sighed and ran a hand over her flyaway hair. Thick and straight, it was as blond now as it had been when she'd been a kid. She knew a lot of women with similar color hair. Not many of them had been born with it.

Had the woman in the underground room been?

Jodie's mind flashed back to the tunnel—the long blond hair lying on the floor, the strands as thick and straight as hers. As thick and straight as her mother's had been.

She shuddered, refusing to let her mind wander further down that path.

She was tired, drained and on edge. Of course she was seeing connections where none existed. A good night's sleep, a little food, and she'd be more rational. At least she'd better be. She had a job to do, a woman to find. She couldn't let anything stand in the way of doing that. Not fatigue. Not hunger. Not the memories that haunted her dreams.

Ten years away. She could have gone a hundred more and been happy about it.

She sighed. If she didn't know better, she'd think being back in Loomis was her punishment for all the Sundays she'd skipped church. Of course, she did know better. God had more important people to work on than Jodie. People who loved Him, sought Him, wanted to know His will.

As for Jodie, she'd spent most of her childhood Sundays sitting in church services that had been filled with sanctimonious people. She didn't plan to spend any more of them doing the same.

Then again, she was back in Loomis. Who was she to say church wasn't in her future?

She almost smiled at the thought, imagining her father's shocked expression if she walked into Loomis Christian Church on Sunday morning. She doubted he'd be happy. As far as Jodie could remember, nothing she'd done had ever met with his approval.

She pulled up in front of the old five-and-dime, parking her car on the street and eyeing the building. A 1940s brick facade with store windows covered by shades, the place had closed when Jodie was a kid and seemed a little worse for wear, the years showing in the faded sign that still hung over the door.

She got out of her car and hurried into the building, not wanting to run into anyone. She needed a cup of coffee and a few minutes alone. Then maybe she'd be ready to face Loomis.

The large space had been set up with several cubicles, each containing a desk and a computer. Jodie bypassed the work area and stepped into a back room that had once been used for storage. Now it contained a long table and a locked file cabinet. A coffee machine sat on a small desk near the wall and Jodie plugged it in, grabbing a foam cup from a stack beside it and waiting impatiently for the coffee to brew.

She sipped the bitter liquid that finally resulted and walked into one of the cubicles, dropping her purse onto the desk and slipping out of her suit jacket. She might as well get to work while she was waiting. Accessing the local PD's computer system was dicey, but she finally managed to get the password from a woman she'd known in high school and who had heard she worked for the FBI.

A search of the open missing persons' cases gave her several possibilities for the identities of the deceased. She printed out a list, excitement thrumming through her as she imagined closing the file on cases that had been in the system for decades. Names for the victims. Faces. Closure for their families.

The thought spurred Jodie on, and she created a spreadsheet listing name, race, age and date missing of each victim.

The door opened, and she turned, smiling, expecting Sam. Instead, she met Harrison Cahill's cool green gaze.

"Are you done at the scene already?"

"Already? It's been almost three hours." His gaze dropped from her face to the sheaf of papers she was holding in her hand, his lips quirking in a sardonic half smile that made her stiffen.

"I guess I lost track of time."

"Hard at work, huh?"

"Isn't that why we're here?" She kept her voice even and refused to look away from his steady gaze. She'd met men like him before. Men who assumed that because she was young she couldn't handle the job and that because she was new she was overly anxious to prove she could. They were wrong on both counts.

"Yeah, I guess it is, but in my experience, the younger the agent, the more anxious she is to show off what she can do."

"Your bluntness is charming, Cahill. But, for the record, I'm not that new and I'm not that young. If my hard work makes you feel inadequate, I'm sorry, but I'm not going to dumb down for anyone."

He blinked, then shook his head and chuckled, the sound as warm and rich as honey from a honeycomb. "Touché, Gilmore. And for the record, you're not making me feel inadequate. You're making me nervous."

"Nervous?"

"Rookies do that to me. Lots of questions. Lots of energy. Lots of impatience. I want to focus on the job, not on walking someone through the process."

"You won't have to walk me through anything. I think I made that clear before."

"I guess you did. So, now that we've both had our say, maybe we can start working together to find out who our victims are. What have you got?"

"Possibilities. I accessed the local PD's missing persons' files. Then I expanded it out to adjoining towns. This is the spreadsheet of open cases." She handed him the printed pages.

"We can rule out more than half of them." He scanned the list, his brow furrowed.

"You know that already?"

"Both victims were Caucasian. Late twenties to early thirties. Hand me a pen, will you?"

Jodie opened the desk drawer, found a pen and handed it to Harrison, her fingers brushing his, warmth shooting up her arm at the contact.

Surprised, she pulled back, watching as he crossed out name after name. "Those two were the correct race and age."

"But not the correct time frame. Our victims were murdered more than two decades ago." He glanced up as he spoke, his eyes the deep green of the bayou and as filled with secrets. "You've got a color printer here, right?"

"I—"

"Yep, you do. Good. You shared with me. Now I'll share with you." He set the marked pages on the desk and slipped a flash drive from his jacket pocket. "These are from my digital camera, downloaded to my laptop. Take a look." He worked quickly, efficiently, with no hesitation. The exact opposite of the careful, meticulous efforts he'd taken at the scene.

Seconds later, photos appeared on the screen. "Here we go. A good pictorial record of what was found. Now I'll print them and give you a copy for your files."

"I appreciate it, but this isn't really an FBI case."

"So Sam told me. The problem is, he's not sure the sheriff is going to investigate the way he should." He lifted the printed photos and handed them to Jodie.

She scanned the photos, the muddy muted colors more a product of the dirt and the dust at the scene than of the quality of printer or camera. Two skulls. Both with visible fractures. Tufts of short dark hair. Longer, blond hair. A gold watch lying near a skeletal outstretched hand. A bracelet. Silver, with several charms attached.

Angel charms?

Her heart skipped a beat, and she squinted at the photo, trying to see more clearly. "Are those angels?"

"Looked that way at the scene. It's not real clear in the

picture, though, is it?" He leaned over her shoulder, looking at the photo, not touching Jodie, though she could feel his warmth through her cotton shirt.

She wanted to move away, put some distance between them. More than that, she wanted to know exactly what was on the charm bracelet. "Was there another charm on it? A mother holding a child? I can't tell from the photo."

"There might have been, but I didn't examine it very closely. Sam brought the evidence to the sheriff. I'll get a better look at it tomorrow and do a more detailed catalog then. Why do you ask?" He stepped away from her shoulder and leaned his hip against the desk, his gaze steady and searching as if he could read the truth in her eyes. See the fear that she didn't dare speak out loud.

"It looks like something I've seen before."

"Yeah? When?"

"I'm not sure." But she was. She'd seen something like it in a picture of her mother that she'd found in a box when she was ten or eleven. The bracelet had been clearly visible, three angels and a mother-and-child charm.

"Then why do you look like you've seen a ghost?"

"What does a person who's seen a ghost look like?" She tried to keep her voice light, but her heart was racing, her gaze drawn again and again to the photo.

"Pale. Shaken. Terrified."

"I'm not terrified. And I'm naturally fair."

"Which still leaves shaken." He searched her eyes, and Jodie's cheeks heated.

"Cahill, I'm not some inexperienced kid who needs to be looked out for. I'm fine."

"No offense, but I'm not worried about your well-being. I'm worried about whether you're withholding information that pertains to my investigation."

"I asked you a question about the bracelet. How does that equate to withholding information?"

"Would you rather have me think that you're too young and inexperienced to handle looking at crime-scene photos." He was baiting her, trying to get her to slip and tell him what was bothering her.

There was no way she would fall into his plan.

Living with her father had taught Jodie plenty about keeping her thoughts to herself. Giving people too much information about how you felt and what you wanted was like giving them the gun and the ammunition they needed to destroy you. Only a fool would do that. And Jodie wasn't a fool. "I've seen a lot worse than those crime scenes when I worked for the Baltimore police." And what I'd rather you do is stick to worrying about identifying your victims."

Harrison looked like he planned to keep pushing for answers, but the door opened and Sam walked in, putting an end to the conversation. "Looks like you two are getting acquainted."

"We were going over crime-scene photos I printed for you. Take a look at this one." He pulled a photo from Jodie's hand and handed it to Sam. "Both skulls had similar wounds to the head. I know for sure one of the victims was shot. I'm pretty confident the other one was, too."

"You're sure?" Sam glanced at the photo, his eyes flashing with interest.

"See the slice in the vertebra there? You take a look, too, Gilmore." He grabbed her hand, pulling her over to look at the photo Sam held. "There's a deep gauge in it."

"I see it." And next to the vertebra more of that white-blond hair. Jodie shuddered and looked away, hoping neither of the men noticed.

"I feel pretty confident that the bullet hit there, cut through the spinal cord and probably lodged somewhere in the diaphragm. I couldn't find evidence of a bullet wound on the other victim, but I'm going to the coroner's office tomorrow to go over the bones in brighter light."

"The MO matches our more recent murders." Sam ran a hand over his cropped hair and frowned. "We should get the results of the DNA test on the blood on Leah Farley's shoe soon. If it's her husband's blood, we'll be looking for a fugitive. If it's hers…"

"You'll be looking for a body." Harrison didn't seem to have any trouble saying what Sam hadn't.

"Right. For now, we'll assume she's alive and that her husband's death isn't related to crimes that happened decades ago."

"I'd say our victims were killed somewhere around twenty-five years ago."

Jodie went cold at Harrison's words but didn't ask what she wanted to. Why twenty-five and not twenty-eight, thirty, twenty-one?

"I've already done a search of missing persons' cases from Loomis and the surrounding area." Jodie managed to get the words out past her tight throat, but her hands trembled as she lifted the pages of information and handed them to Sam.

"Any possible matches?"

"A few." Harrison pointed out the names, but his eyes were on Jodie, his gaze direct and assessing. He'd noticed her re-action to the date he'd given. Just as he'd noticed her reaction to the photo of the bracelet.

She could tell him what she was afraid to voice, but she didn't.

The woman could be anyone.

Or it could be someone she'd known.

Someone she'd loved. Someone she was sure had turned away and never looked back.

Until she had more evidence, she didn't plan to admit that the skeleton could be her mother.

THREE

Jodie paced the room as the men discussed the female victim. She needed to get out of the office. Get away from the photos they'd spread out on the desk. Away from the words she didn't want to hear. The victim was a young woman. Early thirties. Small-boned. Five foot five or six. Probably 115 pounds.

Jodie's height. Jodie's weight. Jodie's bone structure. Jodie's long blond hair.

Could it be a coincidence?

"It's getting late. Let's call it a night and pick this up again tomorrow." Sam sounded as weary as Jodie felt. She couldn't blame him. He'd been in Loomis for two months and barely had any evidence to show for it.

"Sounds good to me." Harrison gathered the photos and handed them to Sam. "You wanted these."

"Right. I'll just file them in my office. See you both tomorrow." He walked to a closed door, unlocked it and disappeared inside.

Jodie didn't wait for a second invitation to end the day. She grabbed her purse and opened the front door, stepping out into the cool night. The rain had stopped, but moisture hung in the air, clogging her lungs.

"Jodie! Hold up a minute." Harrison called out, and Jodie

considered ignoring him. The last thing she wanted was to have another conversation with him.

She stopped anyway, her hand on her car's door. "What's up?"

"Funny, that's exactly what I was going to ask you."

"Nothing is up."

"You ran out of there like the place was on fire."

"It's been a long day. Tomorrow will be even longer."

"Somehow, I don't think that's the real reason you ran." He scanned her face, his eyes seeming almost translucent in the fading light.

"It's one of them."

"And the others?"

"Not something I want to discuss."

"Whatever you know, whatever you're hiding, you're going to have to tell me eventually."

"Maybe, but not today." Because telling Harrison would mean admitting she was scared. More scared than she'd been in a long time. Scared that the woman lying hidden for decades was the mother she'd spent twenty-five years despising, the mother who'd run away and left her three-year-old daughter with a father whose harsh criticisms and cold anger had bordered on abuse.

Harrison searched her face, his brow furrowed. Dark hair, a little too long in the back, brushed his collar as he nodded. "Fair enough, but you may as well know that there are very few secrets the dead can hide from me. I'm not too shabby about getting the truth from the living, either. If what's bothering you has something to do with this case, you won't be able to keep it from me for long."

It was a promise more than a threat, and Jodie sensed that there was nothing arrogant about the words. Harrison Cahill was good at what he did. Great at it, if the little she'd seen was any indication. In other circumstances, she'd be looking forward to seeing more of his methods, watching as he pieced together the puzzle that had been handed to him. But these weren't other circumstances and the sick dread she'd been feeling since she'd first seen those strands of blond hair intensified as Harrison turned and walked back into the building.

She got in her car and drove down Main Street, her mind filled with a million thoughts. None of them good. She'd been told her mother had abandoned her and gone on to live a life free of responsibilities. She'd never doubted that. Maybe she should have.

Jodie needed to talk to her father, ask him what he remembered. Had Amelia told her husband that she planned to leave? Or had she just walked away one day and never returned? As a kid, Jodie had never had the guts to ask, and as an adult she hadn't thought it mattered.

She'd been wrong.

It mattered. A lot. Because someone had been lying dead in the secret room for decades, and that someone just might have been her mother.

Her hands tightened on the steering wheel, and she turned onto the winding road that led to Vera Peel's boardinghouse. Tomorrow, after she'd had time to think, to decide what questions to ask, she'd go to her father's house. For now, she'd rather avoid the confrontation.

The boardinghouse stood on a hill at the edge of town, its gingerbread trim and white porch swing doing little to add cheer or charm to the dark exterior. A painted sign hung from posts in the front yard, the gothic lettering adding a sinister feel to place. Jodie had never been inside the house but had always imagined the interior to be just as uninviting.

She parked her car in the wide, empty driveway, got out and made her way to the porch. The door opened before she even reached the steps, and Vera stepped outside. Tall, spare, with faded red hair and small green eyes, she watched Jodie's approach.

"Hello, Ms. Peel. I was looking for accommodations for the evening. Do you have an empty room?" Of course, Vera did. People might stay at the boardinghouse once, but most never returned.

"No."

"You don't?" Surprised, Jodie paused on the porch stairs.

"That's what I said, isn't it?"

"But I thought—"

"It doesn't matter what you thought, Jodie Gilmore, I don't have a room." Vera's lips were tight with impatience, her eyes flashing with anger. If she remembered Jodie, she also remembered the trouble Jodie had so often been in.

"Ms. Peel, I know I was a troublemaker when I was a kid, but I've grown up. I'm with the FBI now, and—"

"You think I didn't already know that. It's all your dad talks about. His daughter, the big shot FBI agent."

Jodie's father talked about her job? Maybe she'd finally given him something to claim bragging rights over, not that it would matter when she finally saw him face-to-face. Richard Gilmore didn't believe in praising his daughter for anything. As a matter of fact, the only thing he's said when she'd called to tell him she'd been hired by the FBI was, "Don't blow it."

"Then maybe you'll see fit to let me stay for a few days."

"I've got another guest coming. A *man*." She emphasized the last word, her beady eyes gleaming with heated fervor.

"And the rest of your rooms are full?"

"My handyman Chuck stays here, too."

"That's two rooms that are booked. Your house must have several more that are empty."

"What does that have to do with anything? Both of my guests are men. You are a woman. It wouldn't be seemly to have you stay here."

"But, Vera, you run a boardinghouse. You must have had

other times when you've had both male and female guests."
Jodie rubbed the tight muscles in her neck and tried not to let
her impatience show. She needed aspirin for her aching head,
she needed a bed to lie down in, and getting upset with Vera
Peel wouldn't get her either of those.

"I'm sure I have, but I know who you are, Jodie, and I know
where you came from. *Who* you came from." She nearly spat
the words, and Jodie took a step back, almost falling off the step.

"I hope you aren't implying that I can't be trusted around
men because of what my mother did."

"Your mother ran away with another man. Left your father
and you alone. And you know what the Bible says…"

No, but Jodie was sure she was about to find out.

"…the sins of the father are passed down through the third
and fourth generation."

"I don't think that God meant a child should be judged by
her mother's actions."

"I'm sorry, but I really can't let you stay here." Vera gazed
past Jodie, her eyes glittering oddly. "It looks like my guest has
arrived. You'd best be on your way now."

Jodie clenched her teeth to keep from arguing further. Insisting that she wasn't her mother's daughter wouldn't change
Vera's opinion. People in Loomis had decided long ago that
Amelia Pershing Gilmore's daughter was the spitting image of
her mother. Not just in looks but in temperament. Had Jodie
really expected anything more than what Vera had given her?

She turned away from the older woman, hurrying down the
steps as another car pulled in beside hers. A black Jeep with
tinted windows and a glossy exterior. She tried not to resent the
fact that its owner, a complete stranger to Vera, would get a
warmer welcome than she had.

And not just from the owner of the boardinghouse, but also
from almost everyone in town.

She pulled open her car door, started to get in and paused as the Jeep's window slid open.

"Gilmore? You're staying here, too?" Harrison peered out at her, his chiseled face cast in shadows, his eyes gleaming in the darkness. Handsome in a rugged, outdoorsy way. Not the kind of man Jodie usually found attractive. But then, the kind of men she usually went for were too smooth and charming to be trusted.

"No. I…" *Couldn't get a room because my mother was an adulteress?* Of course, she couldn't say that. "I'm staying at my father's."

"Too bad. We could have had a bite to eat together after I unpacked."

"A bite to eat?" Vera's voice was as shrill as a screaming parrot's, her head bobbing as she spoke. "I hope you're not expecting me to feed you, young man. That's not part of what I offer."

"No worries, ma'am, I thought I'd find a place in town."

"And don't think there's coffee at all hours, either. I can't be expected to keep the pot percolating. If you want coffee, you can go to Pershing Provisions for it."

"Understood." Harrison's lips twitched, his eyes dancing with what could only be humor, and Jodie felt her tension draining away. Vera was annoying but harmless. Finding amusement in her antics was a lot better than getting upset about them.

"And no music late at night. No loud phone conversations. No women friends in. Ever." Her gaze cut to Jodie and she scowled, her eyes hard and filled with malice.

"Seems like a lot of rules for a boardinghouse." Harrison pulled a duffel out of his Jeep and started up the steps.

"Follow them or find another place to stay. I've kicked people out of my house before, you know. I won't hesitate to do it again. And I can already tell you that the Loomis Hotel is booked solid. Come in and get the key. I've got other things to do with my time besides chitchatting." She walked inside, and Harrison turned to Jodie.

"This should be an interesting stay."

"Looks that way." But she doubted it would be as interesting as her stay with her father. She hadn't seen the man in ten years and was going to show up on his doorstep and beg for a room. That should be *more* than interesting.

"It'll be even more interesting if you agree to have dinner with me tonight."

"Have dinner with you? You're kidding, right?" Jodie nearly laughed in surprise.

"Why would I be? I'm hungry. I don't want to eat alone."

"You told me earlier that rookies made you nervous. I wouldn't want to ruin your appetite."

"It takes an awful lot to do that." He smiled, and Jodie's breath caught. No man should look that good when he smiled.

"Your appetite might not be affected, but mine would. There is no way can I enjoy a meal when someone is giving me the third degree."

He smiled again, shrugging his shoulders, the soft cotton of his shirt pulling tight against well-muscled shoulders. "I'd be lying if I said I didn't have some more questions for you."

"And I'd be lying if I said I'd answer them."

Harrison laughed and pushed open Vera's front door. "That shouldn't be a reason for us not to have dinner, should it?"

She should say yes, but doing so would mean having to face what she'd much rather avoid—her father. "If we go to dinner, don't expect to get the answers you're looking for."

"Just as long as you don't expect me not to ask them. How about we meet at that Italian restaurant on Main Street."

"Vincetta's?"

"Right. See you there." He stepped inside and closed the door, the evening silence almost eerie in his absence.

Dinner with Harrison Cahill? Probably not the best idea she'd ever had, but that wasn't surprising. Loomis had a way of muddling her thinking. Maybe it was the air—thick with the bayou. Or maybe it was the memories that were always just a whisper away. Either way, the dark and ugly place was already working its magic on her.

She sighed, getting into her car and deciding to make a quick stop at the store to pick up an economy-sized bottle of Tylenol. She had a feeling she was going to need it over the next few days or weeks.

Or months.

Please, God, don't let it be months.

The prayer slipped out, surprising Jodie. It had been a while since she'd thought to ask God for anything. A while since He'd seen fit to answer.

Maybe this time would be different.

Somehow, though, she doubted it.

FOUR

Harrison stood in the large foyer of Vera Peel's boarding-house and glanced around, looking for the proprietress. The FBI had arranged for his stay in the place. He'd have to remember to thank Sam for that.

After he asked him what he'd been thinking.

Harrison had stayed in a lot of small-town bed-and-breakfasts and boardinghouses over the years, but Vera's won the prize for creepiest. Dark. Shadowed. Clean, but grim. Not a restful place, but he'd deal with it.

"I see you finally decided to come in." Vera stepped through a doorway at the end of the hall. Tall and thin, her long dark dress hanging limply from skeletal shoulders, she was as creepy as the house. Maybe more so.

"Sorry I took so long, Mrs. Peel." He smiled and attempted to make nice. After all, he might be staying with the woman for a while.

"I'm sure you're not, but that is not something we need to discuss." She scowled, and Harrison wondered what had happened in her life to make her so prickly. A tough childhood? A bad marriage? Whatever it was, the woman cornered the market on dour.

"Right. If you'll just show me to my room, I'll get out of your hair."

"Here is your key." She thrust an old-fashioned skeleton key at him, and Harrison grabbed it. "Your room is in here." She shoved open a door to the right, flicking on a light. "My other guest is on the second floor, and my room is in the attic. I keep the door locked."

Did she think he'd try to invade her private quarters? The idea would have been laughable if Vera hadn't looked so serious. "Are there any other house rules I should know about? Besides no women and no loud music?"

"Are you mocking me, Mr. Cahill?" She frowned, and Harrison decided the less he saw of his hostess, the better.

"Not at all."

She looked him up and down, her eyes as cold and bleak as the winter sky. "There's a phone in your room. You make long-distance calls, you pay for them."

"Understood."

"Breakfast is at seven. Muffins. Juice. Coffee. You need more than that, you'll have to go elsewhere. Good night, Mr. Cahill." She disappeared down the hall, and Harrison walked into the room, dropping his duffel on the bed. He thought about unpacking but didn't think Jodie would wait at the restaurant for long. There were questions he needed to ask before he continued his investigation. Questions only she could answer.

Like how she'd known that the woman's charm bracelet had angels on it and how she'd known about the mother–child charm.

It took less than ten minutes to drive to the restaurant, and Harrison spotted Jodie's car immediately. A red sports car, it wasn't something he would have picked as hers if he hadn't seen it at Vera's house. Something understated and elegant seemed more her style. Her dark suit, soft makeup and pulled-back hair seemed to reflect a quiet personality.

Of course, Harrison had been wrong about women before. Allison was just the most recent example of that. Thankfully, he'd come to his senses before he made a lifetime commitment to her. A schoolteacher who was as needy as the first graders she taught, she had expected Harrison to give up his freelance work to make time for her. He'd been willing to make time, but not to give up his work. Too bad it had taken him so long to realize that wouldn't be enough.

He frowned, irritated with his train of thought. Allison had broken up with him two years ago, and he hadn't spent much time thinking about her since. He didn't plan to start now. Not when he had a job to do. Two victims. A man and a woman. Dead for more than two decades. Somewhere, people were missing their loved ones. It was Harrison's job to make sure the families would finally have closure.

He pushed open the door to Vincetta's Italian Restaurant and walked inside. The place looked a little fancy for Harrison's taste, but a plate of pasta would fill him just as much as a burger and fries, and Vincetta's was the only decent restaurant he could find in town.

Jodie was already seated in a booth near the far wall, her attention focused on a menu that lay open on the table. Long strands of blond hair had escaped her ponytail and fell across smooth pale skin. Harrison's fingers suddenly itched to brush the strands away, to linger on warm, soft flesh.

He pulled his thoughts up short, surprised by the direction they'd taken. Jodie was a decade younger than he was. Maybe more. He shouldn't be thinking about anything but getting the information he wanted from her. "You look lost in thought," he said as he approached the booth and slid into it, across from her.

She glanced up from the menu, her eyes wide and deep blue, her expression guarded. "Just trying to decide what to eat. It's been a while since I've eaten good Italian."

"It's been a while since I've eaten at all. Seems the last meal I had was sometime before the sun went down last night." He smiled at her, doing his best to seem unthreatening and benign. Jodie was already on guard. If he could get her to relax, he might have a chance at getting the answers he wanted.

"You don't have to make small talk, Cahill. Just cut to the chase, ask your questions and we'll get my refusal to answer them out of the way."

"I'm not sure why you would plan not to answer when what you have to say could help my investigation. Would you care to explain it to me?" He glanced at the menu, then ordered a soda from the waiter who stopped at the table.

"How could anything I have to say help with the investigation?"

"Answering a question with a question. Good tactic, but it's not going to work with me. Something was bothering you today, and it wasn't the crime-scene photos."

"I told you it wasn't."

"But you didn't tell me what it was. If you have information that might help with the investigation, I'd appreciate hearing it."

"I don't." She gestured for the waiter to return for their orders. Obviously she was anxious to get dinner over with.

Harrison wasn't quite as concerned about ending their meal together, and he was honest enough with himself to admit that it wasn't only because he wanted answers. There was something about Jodie that made him want to look and keep looking. Something that made him want to find out more about the young FBI agent.

The very young FBI agent.

He'd do well to keep that in mind. "I think you're lying."

"You can think whatever you want, Cahill. It won't change anything." She had the decency to look uncomfortable, her soft lips turned down, her cheeks pink.

"You think you know the victims, don't you?"

"How could I? I moved away from Loomis ten years ago. I

barely remember my high-school friends, let alone anyone else from town."

"You remembered Vera. And she remembered you."

"Do you think anyone could forget a woman like Vera?"

"I don't think I ever will." He chuckled.

"She's definitely the kind of person who sticks in your brain." Her lips curved, softening her features, making her looking even younger than she had earlier and tempting him to ask just how old she was. He didn't ask, though. The last thing he needed was to put her on the defensive again.

"So she's always been uptight?"

"Ever since her husband left her. Or at least that's what I've been told. I was too young when he left town to remember what Vera was like before. And, like I said, I haven't seen her in ten years. It's possible she's even worse than she used to be."

"Ten years ago. And you were what? Eleven or twelve?" He couldn't help himself, the comment just slipped out.

"Go ahead. Ask." This time Jodie smiled full-out, her eyes dancing with humor, her face relaxed and open and so breathtakingly beautiful Harrison wanted to take out his camera and capture the moment.

"Ask what?"

"How old I am. I know you're dying to."

"I'll admit to mild curiosity."

"Twenty-eight. Not nearly as young as you thought, right?"

She *was* right and probably thought she'd accomplished exactly what she'd planned to—refocusing the direction of the conversation.

Unfortunately for Jodie, Harrison was as tenacious as a bulldog when he got something in his mind. He wouldn't forget her reaction to the photos he showed her or her question about the bracelet, and he wouldn't stop asking about it until he got answers. "Right."

The waiter appeared, setting plates of food down in front of them, then fading back into the restaurant.

Harrison turned his attention back to Jodie.

Despite her effort to appear relaxed, her hands were clenched in fists, her lips tight. She looked anxious. Nervous even. "Of course, I might have been wrong about your age, but I wasn't wrong in thinking that you're hiding something."

"I'm not hiding anything. I'm just…wondering."

"About?"

"How everything is connected. A missing woman. Three recent homicides. The remains of two people left in a boarded-up room for decades."

"Maybe they aren't."

"Do you really think that?"

"The more recent ones probably are, but Jane and John Doe have been dead for at least twenty years. I'm leaning toward thinking their murder is not connected to Loomis's recent crime wave."

"How do you know when they were killed?"

"I recognize the watch we found. It was only made in the 1980s. And it displayed days and months. It gave us a pretty accurate date. It stopped on the eleventh of June."

"It could have stopped years after the murders. I've had watch batteries that run forever."

"It had a windup movement. Probably wound down a couple of days after the murder."

At his words, Jodie blanched, the stark paleness of her face making her eyes glow vivid blue in contrast.

His words had struck a chord with her, and it wasn't a good one.

"June. That's pretty specific." She spoke quietly, her eyes on the plate of pasta she'd barely touched.

"I'm hoping knowing that will give us a quick answer as to who our victims are."

"Quick answers usually aren't easy to come by in our business." They were never easy to come by in Loomis, either. Jodie didn't bother telling Harrison that. Instead, she pushed her plate away, dropped a twenty on the table and stood, more anxious than ever to speak with her father. She wanted to know the day and month her mother had left. A woman with long blond hair and an angel bracelet had been murdered around the same time Jodie's mother had walked away. That didn't mean the two things were connected. It also didn't mean they weren't.

"Running away again, Gilmore?" Harrison rose with her, throwing a twenty down next to his empty plate.

"I'm not running. I'm going to get some sleep so I can tackle all the evidence from a fresh perspective tomorrow."

"Where are you staying?"

"I'm heading to my father's place. Whether or not he'll let me stay remains to be seen."

"I'd think your father would be happy to have you."

"That's because you've never met my father." They stepped outside together, the deep black night barely lit by the restaurant's lights. Rain was in the air, heavy and thick, the chill of it seeping through Jodie's thin suit jacket and cotton shirt. She needed a hot shower, a few hours of sleep. But more than that, she needed answers.

"Just so you know, you're not doing a very good job of making me less curious, Jodie."

"I'm not concerned about your curiosity. I'm concerned about finding the truth." She opened her car door, slid in behind the wheel and said goodbye to Harrison, nervous, on edge and unsure.

She'd been in Loomis for less than twelve hours, and already it was doing its work on her. The woman she'd worked so hard to become, the confident one who never backed down from a challenge seemed to have disappeared. In her place was the in-secure teen Jodie had once been, the frightened child, the young kid who'd wanted desperately to believe that someone, some-where cared about her, praying desperately that she could be good enough to make her father love her.

She shook her head. She'd given up on having her father's love years ago, and she'd given up on God's help long before then. God might answer prayers for other people, but not for Jodie.

Fortunately, she'd learned that going it alone wasn't nearly as difficult as she'd thought it would be.

Sometimes, though, it was awfully lonely.

The thought followed her onto the winding lane that led to her father's house, and it didn't leave as she knocked on the front door of the old colonial and waited for Richard Gilmore to answer.

FIVE

She should have known her father wouldn't answer the door himself. The perky, fortysomething blonde who did, eyed Jodie with a mixture of surprise and curiosity. "Can I help you?"

"Susan?" She hoped she had the right wife. Her father had divorced and remarried several times during her childhood and again after she'd left home.

"Yes."

"I'm Jodie. Your…" She couldn't say stepdaughter since they'd never met. "Richard's daughter."

"Jodie? My goodness! What a surprise! Please, come in." She stepped back, allowing Jodie to move into the large foyer. "I wish I'd known you were coming. I would have had some refreshments for you." Susan brushed a long strand of expertly highlighted hair from her cheek, her nails painted a muted pink, her makeup perfectly applied. A typical Richard woman. Put together. Pretty. Quiet and charming. Decades younger than he was.

"I should have called first."

"Of course you shouldn't have. I'm so happy you're here. Come into the solarium. Your father is reading the pa—"

"What's all the commotion out here? Can't a man get a few minutes of quiet when he gets home from work?"

Jodie tensed as the door at the end of the hall opened and

her father appeared. He hadn't changed much. His dark hair was a little more gray, his face a little more lined, his stomach larger, but he still carried himself with authority, his back straight, his movements impatient.

His eyes widened as he caught sight of Jodie, his lips tightening into a thin line. He wasn't happy to see her. But, then, she hadn't expected him to be.

"Hi, Dad."

"Jodie. What are you doing back in town?"

"Working. The FBI called me in to help with a case."

"That Leah Farley woman's disappearance?" Richard scowled and ran a hand over his military-short hair.

"Yes."

"A waste of time and taxpayer's money. The woman ran off on her husband and kid just like your mother did."

"Only when she left, her husband was dead." Jodie watched her father, gauging his reaction to her comment. Sam had called her in to get information from Loomis residents. She might as well begin with her father.

"Most people say he deserved to be." Susan spoke quietly, her gaze darting from Jodie to Richard and back again.

"Why would they say that?" Jodie hoped her father didn't decide to cut off the conversation before it took wing. Richard had a way of killing any topic he wasn't interested in. At least he had when she'd been a kid. Maybe he'd changed.

Right. Sure he had.

"Earl wasn't always a very good husband. The way I hear it, he used to yell something fierce. Why—"

"Susan, how about you get us some coffee and some of those chocolate-chip cookies you made yesterday? We'll have them in the solarium. Come on, Jodie. I'm sure we've got plenty to talk about." Richard walked away, not giving either woman time to suggest another plan.

That was pure Richard. Arrogant. Thoughtless. How so many women had fallen in love with her father was something Jodie hadn't ever been able to figure out.

"I really don't need coffee or cookies." She followed him into the solarium, the dark leather furniture and book-lined shelves reflecting much more of his personality than it seemed to reflect Susan's.

"I do. Besides, Susan has too much time on her hands, and she spends most of it gossiping. Or spending my money."

"It isn't gossip when it's helping with an investigation." She tried to get the conversation back on track.

"Helping with what investigation? The FBI has been here for two months. In that time, three people have turned up dead and the woman the FBI came to find is still missing. It's a waste of taxpayer's money to have you people here. Let Sheriff Reed handle things. That's what I said from the beginning, and I haven't changed my mind." He settled into a leather recliner and gestured for Jodie to take a seat.

"If the people in town were more forthcoming with information, the case might be closed by now."

"If the agents who were working the case spent more time asking questions and less time romancing local women, maybe people around here would be more forthcoming." Richard scowled, his voice rising on the last few words.

Great. She'd been in the house less than fifteen minutes and she'd already brought out the worst in her father. No surprise there. She's spent half her childhood trying to figure out how not to provoke her dad's temper. The other half she'd spent seeing just how angry she could make him.

"No need to raise your voice, Dad. I came to do my job. Not to aggravate you."

"What? The FBI was so desperate it had to call in a nobody

to get the job done?" It was a low blow, one that would have sent Jodie running years ago. Now, she let it slide off her.

"They wanted someone who was familiar with the people in Loomis. They're hoping that will open the lines of communication."

"Fat chance you could do that for them." Richard's light blue eyes probed hers, and Jodie was sure he was looking for some sign that his words had affected her. She wouldn't give it to him.

"We'll see what I can do, Dad. For now, I was hoping I could stay here for the duration of the investigation."

"You're gone for ten years, and you think Sue and I will open our home to you just like that? A little notice would have been nice."

"I'd planned to stay at the hotel, but it's booked solid. Vera doesn't have room, either."

"Then I guess we've got no choice but to put you up."

"You don't have to do anything, Dad. If you'd rather I stay somewhere else, I'm sure I can find someone willing to give me a place to stay for a while. Maybe one of the Pershings will." She wasn't sure of any such thing. Her father had kept her cut off from her mother's family, refusing to allow visits. None of the Pershings had seemed to care enough to demand them.

"Of course you can stay with us, Jodie." Susan stepped into the room, her deep brown eyes showing warmth.

"This is my house, and I—"

"*Our* house, Rich. Wasn't that what you said to me when I wanted to buy a new house to start our lives together?" Susan smiled sweetly, but Jodie sensed the steel beneath the expression. Maybe, for the first time ever, her father had met his match.

"Well, of course it's our house, but Jodie—"

"Is your daughter and you haven't seen her in years. I, for one, am excited to have her here." Susan set a tray of coffee and cookies on a small side table and smiled at Jodie.

"I appreciate that, Susan, but I don't want to put either of you out."

"How could it possibly be putting us out? Besides, having you here will give the bridge ladies something to talk about besides the Mother of the Year contest and pageant. Let me just say that it's not easy being a childless woman in this town."

"I understand. Being a motherless child wasn't much fun, either." The comment slipped out before Jodie thought it through, and her father sent a sharp look in her direction.

"What do you mean 'motherless'? There was always a woman in this house when you were growing up."

"True, but it would have been nicer if Mom had stuck around."

Her heart beat faster as she said words she never would have dared a decade ago. Her father might not have information about Leah Farley, but he certainly knew more about Jodie's mother.

"Amelia had bigger fish to fry than me, you or this little town. There was no way she planned to stick around."

"When was it that she left? Wasn't it right before my birthday?"

"Your birthday is in November—"

"December."

"Right. December. Amelia left in the summer."

A cold chill raced up Jodie's spine at his words, and she leaned toward him. "When in the summer? June? July? August?"

"You expect me to remember something that happened twenty-five years ago?"

"When it was something that big, yeah."

"It might be big to you, but it isn't to me."

The words were like a slap in the face, and Jodie could think of nothing to say in reply. Fortunately, Susan had enough words for both of them.

"Richard, you haven't seen your daughter in ten years. Would it really kill you to be a little kinder to her?"

"What's not kind about what I said? Amelia cheated on me, divorced me and ran off with the guy she'd been having an affair with. I've done everything I can to forget that part of my life."

"I understand, sweetheart, but I'm sure Jodie would like some answers about what happened. She was too young to remember much about her mother." Susan settled into a chair next to Richard's, and Jodie bit back a sigh of resignation. She knew her father wouldn't add to what he'd already said, and Susan's unknowing comment would only send him on another one of his rants.

"What answers? Amelia signed the divorce papers on a Saturday and was gone by Monday."

"You can remember what day she left town but not what month?" Jodie asked the question knowing that she wouldn't get an answer.

"I can't tell you either with any certainty. I had my hands full taking care of you. I didn't have time to think about days and seasons. If Amelia hadn't been so selfish, we could have shared the burden of responsibility."

"Do you think that's what it was about? Mom not wanting to take responsibility for me?"

"For you? For anything." Richard took a sip of coffee, so relaxed they could have been talking about anything or anyone. Obviously, he had gone on with his life in a way Jodie had never been able to do.

She stood, suddenly anxious to end the conversation. There'd be time to get the answers she needed. Plenty of people in Loomis remembered her mother. If pressed, they'd tell her what she wanted to know. "It's been a busy day. If the two of you don't mind, I think I'd like to settle down for the night."

"Oh, of course. We'll put you in the guest room. Do you have a bag? Richard, go get her bag and bring it up." Susan spoke as she led Jodie out of the solarium. To Jodie's surprise, her father asked for her car keys and went out to get her bag.

Maybe he'd been more anxious to end the conversation about Amelia than Jodie had thought.

She followed Susan up the stairs and into a room that was once her father's study. Now it was decorated in sage and cream, the old beige carpet pulled up to reveal refinished oak floors. Nicked and stained from time and use, the floor only added to the comfortable feel of the room. "It's lovely, Susan. You've done a great job in here."

"Actually, your father's third wife did this. It was so beautiful, I decided to leave it."

"Sorry. I wasn't thinking."

"No need to apologize. I know I'm not the first Mrs. Gilmore. I plan on being the last, though. There's a bathroom through here. I don't think it was like that when you left."

No. It wasn't. The room on the other side of the closet wall had once been her bedroom. "Thanks, Susan. I really appreciate you putting me up like this."

"No need to thank me. I'm just glad you're here. Your father talks about you all the time. He's so proud of what you've accomplished."

You've got to be kidding.

The words almost slipped out, but Jodie didn't let them. She didn't know much about Susan, and she didn't want to offend her. Maybe she really did think Richard loved his daughter. "I guess having an FBI agent as a daughter is big news in Loomis."

"It *was* big news. With everything that's happened lately, it's lost some of its edge. Don't worry, though. Once things calm down, I'm sure your job will be back on top of the list of things to discuss." Susan was serious, her pretty face and deep brown eyes full of sincerity.

"I guess people in town must be nervous, what with the murders that have happened here."

"We're certainly making sure the doors and windows are locked. Although most people think Dylan, Angelina and Earl were involved in something illegal." She whispered the last word, glancing around as if someone else might be close enough to hear.

"In other words, they got involved in something that got them killed."

"Why else would they all be murdered? Loomis isn't a crime-ridden community. Things like this just don't happen without a reason."

"You could be right, Susan. That's what I'm here to find out." She planned to ask Susan what she knew of Leah and Earl Farley's relationship, but her father appeared in the bedroom door, her duffel bag in hand.

"Here it is. Did you bother packing any appropriate work clothes? Or did you just shove in makeup and hair gels?" He scowled as he tossed the bag onto the bed.

"I'm almost thirty years old, Dad. You don't need to worry about what I'm going to wear to work."

"Fathers always worry, Jodie," Susan said lightly. "Come on, honey. Let's let your daughter rest. I'm sure she's got a busy day ahead of her tomorrow." She smiled kindly as she took Richard's hand and tugged him back out the door.

It closed with a soft click, and Jodie relaxed for the first time since she'd set foot in the house. At least when she was alone she didn't have to worry about answering Susan's questions or parrying her father's next attack.

She unpacked quickly, hanging pants and blouses in the closet before changing and getting into bed. With the light off and the house silent around her, she stared up at the ceiling, willing away the whispered memories that seemed to fill the dark room. A hint of perfume, a quiet song, a pale face peering out from beyond the bathroom door. Nothing concrete or real. How could there be? What Jodie remembered about her mother came from seeing photographs and hearing stories. Sometimes she wished she had her own memories of the woman who'd given birth to her. Other times she was glad she didn't. It was hard to miss what she couldn't remember having.

She sighed, turning over on the bed and closing her eyes. She did miss it, though. Having Susan treat her like she belonged only reminded her of what she'd never had and probably never would. Family. Affection. A place to call home.

Not that Jodie needed those things. She'd been going it alone since she'd left Loomis at eighteen. She planned to keep going it alone. Counting on other people would only lead to disappointment, and she'd had enough of that when she was a kid to last a lifetime.

SIX

Jodie's cell phone rang before the sun came up the next day. She grabbed it from the bedside table and answered without glancing at the caller ID. "Gilmore here."

"I hope you're up and ready to start your day, because I need you to meet me in ten minutes." Sam's voice filled the line, gritty and hard.

"At headquarters?"

"No. At 1645 Swamp Way. A woman there has just found a threatening note on her car."

"And she called the FBI?" Jodie shoved aside blankets and jumped out of bed.

"She called the sheriff's department. Sheriff Reed responded, saw the note and called me."

"Does the note have something to do with our missing person's case?" Jodie couldn't imagine any other reason to be called to something that should have been handled by local police.

"The sheriff thinks so. I'm going to withhold an opinion until after I see the note."

"You think he's off base?"

"I think he likes to say *jump* and see how high I'll go."

"I'll be there in ten." Jodie hung up the phone and hurried to shower and dress. Black slacks, white button-down shirt, black jacket. Nothing too frilly or feminine. She pulled her hair back into a low ponytail, long strands of it sliding over her shoulder as she applied her makeup. Blond hair against dark fabric. It reminded her of the skeleton that had been found the previous day, the long, straight hair that had looked as blond as Jodie's, her father's comment about her mother leaving in the summer.

She shook her head, not wanting to acknowledge what she feared. It *wasn't* her mother that had been lying there for all those years. She couldn't shake the worry that gnawed at her as she drove to meet Sam.

He and Sheriff Reed stood next to a minivan, eyeing a petite brunette who stood next to it. Sam glanced Jodie's way as she got out of her car. "Agent Gilmore, this is Jillian Morrison. She found a note on her car when she came out to go to work. Take a look."

He handed her a note that was already sealed in a plastic bag, the words clearly visible, the deep red blood bright against the stark white paper. "Drop out of the pageant unless you want to end up dead like Dylan Renault or gone like Leah Farley."

She glanced at the woman. Midthirties, attractive, well dressed. "You've been nominated for Mother of the Year?"

"Yes. This is my third year being nominated. Last year, I won." Unlike most of the winners Jodie remembered from her childhood, Jillian didn't seem overly proud of the accomplishment.

"Congratulations."

Jillian shrugged. "Every mother deserves to be honored for what she does."

"When did the list of nominees go out?"

"A week ago."

"So everyone in town knows you were on it?"

"Everyone who is interested in the pageant."

"Has anyone else received a note like this?" Jodie directed the question at Sheriff Reed, who looked like he'd rather have stayed in bed than report to the scene.

"If someone had, I would have called Agent Pierce. This is the first one we got. 'Course, that doesn't mean it's going to be the last."

"When did you get home last night, ma'am?" Sam cut in, and Jodie walked around the side of the car, searching for subtle evidence. A cigarette, a piece of paper, a footprint in the wet earth. She saw nothing.

"My son and I got home from his physical-therapy session at six-thirty."

"How about your husband?"

"He passed away three years ago. If you were wondering if anyone might have come home later than I did, the answer is no. I pulled into the driveway and parked the car, went into the house and didn't come out again until this morning."

"Did you hear anything? A car, maybe?" Jodie knew the answer before she asked, but she had to ask anyway.

"No. I sleep at the back of the house." Jillian sighed. "Look, I know there's not much y'all can do to help find the person who did this. I just thought I should report it. I've really got to get my son to school, so unless there's something else…"

"We're fine, Jillian. We need anything else from you, we'll let you know. You go ahead and get Marcus." Sheriff Reed made the decision without consulting Sam, and Jillian hurried into the house.

As soon as the door closed, he started toward his cruiser, calling over his shoulder as he went. "Looks like we're done here. I'll let you know if we get any more calls like this one."

He drove away, and Sam frowned. "Were we done here?"

"I was thinking we weren't."

"Me, too. So, how about we separate? You go to the house on the left. I'll go to the one on the right. Maybe one of the neighbors saw or heard something."

Go knock on the neighbors' doors? In any other town, Jodie

would have thought nothing of knocking on doors and questioning people, but this wasn't any other town. It was Loomis. People here knew Jodie. Or had known her. And what they'd known her as was a scrawny wild child, who'd wandered the neighborhood getting into trouble.

She knocked on the first door, bracing herself as it opened and a tall white-haired man peered out at her. "Jodie Gilmore. All grown up and an FBI agent."

It took a minute for her to place him. "Mr. Hillshire?" James Hillshire worked at the library when Jodie lived in Loomis and had always been kind to her when she'd gone to lose herself in books.

"Who else?"

"Sorry. It's been a few years since I visited the Loomis Public Library."

"Been two since I was librarian there. Come on in for a minute. Have a visit." He smiled broadly and gestured for her to come inside.

"Actually, Mr. Hillshire, I just want—"

But he was already inside the house, giving her no choice but to follow.

"Been a lot of stuff going on around these parts." He led her down a hall and into a small kitchen. "Coffee?"

"No, thanks."

"I hear you're in town looking for that Leah Farley woman."

"Did you know her?"

"About as well as most people. She was a nice young lady. Loved her kid."

"And her husband?"

"Now, that's something I can't say. I suppose, like any couple, they had their problems."

"Have you heard anyone say where she might have gone?"

"Not a word. Unless you count rumors. I don't."

"Rumors are usually based on fact."

"Maybe so, Jodie, but you know I'm not one to repeat things."

"I understand, Mr. Hillshire, but your next-door neighbor received a threatening note this morning, and the FBI is concerned it might be connected to Leah's disappearance. Any information you have will be appreciated."

"A threatening note, huh? I thought something was going on over there. She and the boy okay?"

"They're fine."

"Good. Good. Jillian has been through a lot the last few years, what with her husband dying of a heart attack so young. The boy was born with problems, you know. Cerebral palsy. Can't even walk."

"No, I didn't."

"She loves that boy. Works hard to make sure he's got the best chance he can for a good life. It's why she won Mother of the Year last year. Probably will win it again this year."

"If someone doesn't scare her into dropping out."

"People around this town sure do take that contest seriously. Doesn't surprise me that someone threatened Jillian to get her to drop out."

"Did you hear anything last night?"

"Nothing, but then my hearing isn't as good as it used to be."

"Is there anyone you can think of who might want to win badly enough to threaten another mother?"

"Jodie, I can think of a half-dozen women in this town who'd be willing to threaten another Mother of the Year nominee. I don't think any of them would follow through, though."

"Maybe not, but three people in town are dead and a woman is missing. So someone in town is capable of following through on a threat."

"You're right there, but don't ask me who. Leah Farley was well liked. Her husband, Earl, not so much. Dylan Renault…"

He shrugged. "Well, you know what people think of the Renaults."

"And the other victim? The woman?"

"She had a reputation, but who doesn't in this town? That's the extent of what I know. I wish I could offer more, Jodie."

"You've given me plenty to think about. You can reach me at my father's house if you think of anything else. Or call me on my cell phone." She handed him a business card and walked back down the hall toward the front door. She hesitated before she opened it, knowing she shouldn't ask the question that was on her mind but helpless to stop herself from doing it.

"Mr. Hillshire, you knew my mother, didn't you?"

"Sure did. She was a sweet young lady. Loved to read. Just like you."

"Do you remember the year she left?"

"Remember? How could I forget? People still bring it up every now and again. How she signed the divorce papers and walked away two days later. Everyone could understand her turning her back on Loomis and on your father, but no one could figure out why she turned her back on…" His voice trailed off. "Sorry. That was thoughtless of me."

"No need to apologize. It was a long time ago." But it still hurt. No matter how much she tried to tell herself it didn't.

"Why were you asking about your mother?"

"Coming back to town made me think about her. She left in the summer, right?" She didn't tell him about the remains that had been found the previous day. News had probably already spread, but she wouldn't be part of it.

"That's right."

"Do you remember what month?"

"I'm afraid I don't. Sorry."

"It's okay. I've got to go. Thanks for the information."

"Come by and see me again sometime, you hear?"

Jodie nodded, stepping outside and waving goodbye.

The conversation had lasted ten minutes and had yielded little in the way of new information. She hadn't expected it to, but she'd hoped.

"Get anything?" Sam strode toward her, and she walked forward to meet him.

"Nothing that we didn't already know."

"Same here. I'm meeting a friend for breakfast. Why don't we meet at headquarters in an hour and go over our notes."

"Sounds good." She thought about getting some breakfast before going to headquarters, but didn't. She wanted to look at the photos again, see if she'd missed something when she looked at them the day before. Some clue that would tell her for sure that Jane Doe wasn't her mother.

Or that she was.

"Enough. Focus on the missing person's case. That's why you're here." She spoke out loud as she got in her car and put it into Drive, but no matter how hard she tried she couldn't stop picturing the strands of long hair and the delicate angel bracelet.

Her mother's?

She didn't know, but she planned to find out, because no matter how much she wanted to deny it, the past had everything to do with the present. Until she faced it, she would never truly be free of Loomis.

SEVEN

Not hungry enough to eat, too wound up to go back to her father's house, Jodie drove straight to headquarters. A black Jeep was parked in front of the building, and Jodie recognized it immediately. Harrison.

She hadn't expected to see him so early. Why, she didn't know. He'd worked with single-minded determination the day before, his interest in the scene and in the victims obvious.

Maybe she'd just *hoped* she wouldn't see him so early. She hadn't slept well and felt groggy from it. The last thing she needed was another bout of question-and-evasion with Harrison.

She got out of her car anyway, pushing open the office door, the sharp scent of coffee brightening her mood. A little caffeine and she'd feel better about things.

"You're here early." Harrison stepped out of the back room, his hair mussed, his jaw shadowed with the beginning of a beard. As she glanced at him, Jodie's heart had the nerve to skip a beat.

She ignored it, dropping her purse on the desk she'd used the day before. "I could say the same about you."

"The earlier I arrive at work, the quieter it is." His voice was gruff, his face set. Obviously, he was annoyed at her presence.

"Is that a hint that you'd rather I leave?"

"I don't hint. If I wanted you to go, I'd say so."

"And you really think I'd listen?"

"I didn't say you'd listen. I just said I'd tell you." He smiled, the gruffness easing from his voice. "In case you're interested, I brewed a fresh pot of coffee."

"A fresh pot? How long have you been here?" She moved past him as she walked to the back room, the scent of coffee mixing with something subtle and masculine. Shampoo. Soap. *Harrison*. She shouldn't be noticing, but seemed helpless not to.

"A few hours."

"I guess you're as anxious to close this case and put Loomis behind you as I am." The words slipped out, and Jodie was sure Harrison would comment on them.

Instead, he leaned against the doorjamb, his gaze unwavering as she poured coffee into a foam cup and took a sip.

"You're staring."

"Just thinking you've got a lot of secrets and that I wouldn't mind if you shared a few."

"Secrets? I work for the FBI. My life is an open book."

"But your thoughts aren't."

"What I'm thinking is that I need to get some more coffee into me before Sam gets here and the workday officially begins. How is that for a deep dark secret?" She took another sip of the steaming brew, allowing the bitter heat of it to slide down her throat and warm the chill that she'd been feeling since she'd seen the long blond hair of their Jane Doe.

"Not nearly as interesting as the evidence I've got here. Come take a look." He straightened, crossing the room to a long table that had been set up near the far wall. Several items were lined up there, and a laptop computer sat on a desk nearby.

Jodie stepped closer, scanning the items. Bits of cloth. A leather belt. No bracelet. "You've been working hard."

"That's the only way to do it. I'll be heading over to the coroner's later to start reconstruction on the victims' faces. Right now, I'm looking at the evidence I collected yesterday."

"I thought it was at Sheriff Reed's office."

"It was, but the on-duty officer was willing to let me take it." He slipped on gloves and lifted a gold watch from a manila envelope. "This is the watch I was telling you about. Expensive piece. Swiss. The month and day are here. June eleventh.

"And you're sure about how old it is?"

"Based on the style of watch, combined with the level of decomposition, both organic and synthetic, I'd say it's about twenty-five years old. We're within five years of that for the date of the crime."

"So, it could have happened twenty or thirty years ago?"

"You seem awfully concerned about the dates." His eyes glowed with green fire as he watched her, studied her, trying to see the secrets she wasn't ready to reveal.

"The closer we are date-wise, the easier it will be to identify our victims," Jodie glanced away. "What else have you got?"

He eyed her for a moment, his gaze as dark and mysterious as the bayou.

Finally, he shrugged, dropping the watch back into the envelope.

"Not much. Here's the bracelet I found." He picked up another envelope and dumped the contents into his palm. Silver glinted in the overhead light, delicate. Beautiful. Three angel charms and one that was different. A mother holding her child.

Jodie's head spun, and she put her hand on the table, swaying as the world tilted beneath her.

"What is it, Gilmore?" Harrison's palm pressed against her back, holding her steady, anchoring her in the present.

She knew she had to tell him.

She might not want to discuss her mother, might not want

to think about Amelia lying dead in that room, but Jodie couldn't withhold information that could potentially help identify the victims.

"My mother had a bracelet like that."

"Had? Did she lose it? If so, it's possible someone she knew took it. We—"

"My mother has been gone for twenty-five years. She left when I was three, and I haven't seen or heard from her since."

"Twenty-five years?" His brow furrowed, and he stared down at the silver bracelet, examining it closely before dropping it back into the envelope. Then he met Jodie's gaze, his eyes so filled with compassion that Jodie had to look away. "Do you know what time of year it was when she left?"

"Summer. I don't have a firm date, but I can get it. She and my father had just signed divorce papers. Before the ink was dry, she was gone."

"To be with another man?"

"So the story goes. I've never been one hundred percent sure, though. My father was the one who told it. The rest of the town chose to believe him."

Harrison nodded, pulling open a file cabinet and taking out the photos he'd printed the previous day. "Blond hair. I didn't think about it, but it's a lot like yours."

The words were like a blow to the stomach, and Jodie tensed from it. "There are a lot of people in the world with blond hair."

Harrison looked up from the photos, a frown pulling at his lips and creasing his forehead. "You're as white as a ghost. Sit down, Jodie, before you fall down."

"I'm not going to fall down." But she sat anyway, afraid she might do just what he'd said and keel over.

Harrison ran a hand over his hair and tried to control the adrenaline that was racing through him. He had a lead. A good one. He wanted to run with it. But he also had Jodie, and she wasn't looking too steady. Dealing with that came before following up on the information she'd just handed him.

He pulled a chair over and sat down across from her, taking her cool, dry hand in his, treating her as he'd treated the families of any of the victims he'd identified over the years.

"You're right. There are plenty of women in the world with blond hair. And the charm bracelet is pretty generic. There's every chance your mother isn't the woman we found."

"And every chance she is." She took a shuddering breath and tugged her hand from his, her expression changing. Going from shock and horror to professional indifference.

She might look delicate and ethereal, but Jodie was tough. Harrison could see it in the intensity of her gaze as she stood and moved back to the table. "Can you get DNA from the remains?"

"Probably."

"Then take mine, too. If there's a match, we'll have our answer."

Part of the answer, anyway. They'd still have another victim to identify. Another part of the story to figure out.

Harrison didn't remind Jodie of the fact. She had enough to think about. Enough to deal with. "I'll ask the sheriff if he's got the DNA kit. If not, I'll have my office in New Orleans send me one."

"Let me know when you've got it." She brushed a strand of hair from her cheek, her hand trembling, her eyes ocean blue and filled with the anxiety she didn't allow to show on her face.

Tough. Strong. Controlled.

Had Loomis made her that way?

Despite the peaceful location and scenic views, the town had a dark undertone, one that Harrison found disturbing. He couldn't imagine spending another few days here, let alone weeks, months or years. "It shouldn't be long. A day, tops."

"And then another month before the testing is complete?" She asked, but Harrison knew she didn't really be need to be told. She'd dealt with DNA evidence before, but if keeping their professional dialogue going made her feel better, he was happy to oblige.

"I've got some contacts. I'll make sure it's expedited."

"I appreciate that." She tried to smile, but the hollowness in her eyes stole any warmth from the expression. "I think I'll go get some breakfast."

She stepped toward the door, and Harrison knew he should let her leave. If she were any other woman, if this were any other case, he would. But there was something about Jodie that tugged at his heart. Maybe it was her strength. Maybe it was the sadness he saw when he looked into her eyes. Or maybe it was simply because she seemed young and vulnerable and alone.

He grabbed her hand, tugging her to a stop before she could make her escape. "Are you okay, Gilmore?"

"Why wouldn't I be?"

"Because one of the victims we're dealing with might be your mother."

"I haven't seen my mother in twenty-five years. I barely re-member her."

"That doesn't mean it won't hurt if I discover that she's our Jane Doe."

"It'll hurt, Harrison, but I've survived a lot worse. Now, I really do have to get something to eat." She pulled away from his hold and hurried away.

Harrison watched her go, knowing he shouldn't follow but wanting to anyway. Jodie was an enigma. Hard and soft. Tough and vulnerable. A puzzle that he wanted to solve.

He frowned, not liking the direction of his thoughts.

His life was too busy and too complicated already. Adding more to it wasn't part of his plan. The sooner he solved this case and put Jodie Gilmore and her sad-eyed gaze behind him, the happier he'd be. With that in mind, he dialed the sheriff's office, determined to get a DNA test kit and get back to work and even more determined to put Jodie out of his thoughts.

Unfortunately, he wasn't sure that would be nearly as easy as he wanted it to be.

He frowned again. If familiarity bred contempt, maybe the key to getting Jodie out of his head was as simple as spending more time with her. He grabbed his keys, locked the evidence room and followed her outside, praying he wasn't making a big mistake, pretty certain he was and not quite sure he cared.

EIGHT

Food was the last thing Jodie wanted, but she unlocked her car door anyway. No way was she going to stay at headquarters with Harrison. His compassionate gaze and warm touch made her feel things she'd never felt before: Protected. Cared for. Vulnerable and needy.

So many things she didn't want to be.

Years spent listening to her father's verbal abuse had toughened her. She liked it that way. No way would she ever be as sensitive as she'd been when she was a girl and every unkind word had cut deeply.

"I think I'll join you for breakfast." Harrison's deep voice carried across the parking lot, pulling Jodie from her thoughts.

She glanced over her shoulder, saw him moving toward her, his stride long and determined, his face all sharp angles and hard planes. Handsome. Driven. The kind of man who would want his way in everything. A lot like her father.

"Actually, I'm not as hungry as I thought. I'm going to…" *What?* She needed an excuse, but she couldn't think of one. There was nowhere she wanted to go, no one she wanted to see. Not in Loomis anyway.

"What?" Harrison echoed her silent question, a half smile softening his hard features. Flecks of gold in his eyes seemed to reflect the sun's rays, and for a moment Jodie felt caught in his gaze, held captive by the warmth she saw there.

She blinked, turning away and pulling open her car door. There were plenty of things she could do with her time. Things that would get the investigation moving toward its conclusion. "I'm going to Renault Corporation. Dylan Renault was murdered a few weeks ago. I want to discuss his death with his family."

"It's a little early in the morning for that, isn't it?"

Probably, but she wouldn't admit it. "If no one is there, I'll head back here."

"So, you're really not getting anything to eat?" He looked so disappointed, Jodie smiled.

"I'm really not."

"Too bad. Vera's idea of breakfast is a stale muffin and cold coffee."

"Whatever is cheapest. That's Vera Peel. At least that's what people always said about her."

"Yeah, well, she takes cheap to a new level. She informed me this morning that if I had my lights on until 2:00 a.m., she'd have to charge me extra to pay for the electricity."

"Doesn't it send shivers down your spine imagining her lurking outside your room at night?"

"Did you have to put that image in my head?" He scowled, but there was a hint of humor in his eyes.

"Sorry."

"No, you're not. And I don't think you're worried about me going hungry, either."

"There is a little diner in town that serves a pretty good breakfast."

"Good. Let's go." He rounded her car and was in the passenger seat before she realized what he was up to.

Surprised, she opened her door and leaned down to stare him in the eye. "This isn't a good idea, Harrison."

"Why not? I'm hungry, and you obviously need to eat."

"What's that supposed to mean?" Miffed, she slid into the car and thought about pushing him out his still-open door. She figured him at about six-one, maybe 190 pounds. Most of it muscle. He outweighed her, but she was probably faster.

"It means you're scrawny."

Okay, that did it. She was going to shove him out the open door. "Look, Harrison, I don't know what your game is, but—"

"I don't play games, Jodie. I'm hungry. I want breakfast. I want answers, too. I figure if I eat with you, I can kill two birds with one stone."

"Answers to what? Who Jane and John Doe are? I can't help you with that any more than I already have." She put the car in gear and peeled out of the parking lot, not caring that Sheriff Reed was probably lurking somewhere nearby waiting for her to mess up like she had so many times when she was a teen.

"I think there's more information you can give me. As much as I hate to ask, I've got to."

"Go ahead." *Because, really, what choice did she have but to answer?*

"You said your mother left your father for another man. Do you know who that man was?"

Jodie's hands tightened on the steering wheel, and she gritted her teeth. "How would I know? I was three when she left."

"Loomis is a small town. I imagine a lot of people would have known about the affair. I doubt they kept quiet about it."

He was right, of course. There'd been plenty of talk about Amelia Pershing Gilmore's affair. In a town where motherhood was valued above everything but money and God, abandoning a child for a man was big news. Jodie had spent most of her elementary school years hiding from the playground bullies who'd heard the story from their parents and who loved nothing better than to taunt her with it.

Middle school was worse. There, she became the target of a different kind of bullying.

"Hey, are you okay? You're looking pale again." Harrison's hand rested on her arm, the warmth of it seeping through her buttoned down shirt, reminding her that the past was only a memory and that the kid she'd been was gone.

"I've spent ten years trying to put the past behind me. Now, here I am, right back in the middle of it again." She tried to keep her tone light, but knew she'd failed.

"I'm sorry. I know this is painful for you." He squeezed her arm lightly, then released his hold.

She should have been glad, but wasn't. His touch had anchored her to the present. Without it, she was afraid she'd be pulled back into the past. Into the fear and insecurity. Into the darkness that had seemed to be so much a part of her teenage years.

She shook her head, disgusted by her weakness. She didn't need Harrison Cahill's hand on her arm to keep her grounded. And she didn't need to pretend the past hadn't happened to be okay right now.

She took a deep steadying breath. "To answer your question, I don't think anyone in town knows who my mother had an affair with. Like you said, if they did, I think I would have heard about it." She pulled into the parking lot of a small diner at the edge of town. "Here we are. You've got twenty minutes, Cahill. That's all the time I've got before I go back to headquarters."

"I thought we were going to the Renault Corporation?" He got out of the car and followed her across the nearly full parking lot.

"I'll drop you off, then go." The sooner she got Harrison back to the office and out of her hair, the happier she'd be.

"Too bad. Sheriff Reed said that if someone in town had owned an expensive Swiss watch, Charla Renault would remember it. I thought I'd ask her about it."

"You should. Charla's got an eye for anything that's worth

anything. A friend of mine got engaged a month before she graduated high school. Her boyfriend was older. He'd just graduated college, and he gave her a beautiful one-karat diamond solitaire. Told her he'd paid a year's salary for it. Charla got a look at it and declared it a fake."

"Was it?"

"Faker than blond hair on a brunette."

Harrison laughed, holding open the door to the diner. "You sounded like a true Southerner just then."

"I am a true Southerner. I've just worked hard to get rid of the accent."

"Why?"

Because she hadn't wanted any remainders of the life she'd lived in Loomis. "My accent was so thick, people up north couldn't understand me half the time."

"That's right. You said you were a police officer in Baltimore." He took her elbow, urging her across the room to an empty table against the wall. "This looks good. I already know what I want. How about you?"

"You haven't even looked at a menu."

"We don't have a lot of time, and I figure any diner worth its salt has eggs, sausage and biscuits." He waved a waitress over, giving her his order and tapping his fingers impatiently while Jodie looked over the menu.

She ordered coffee and toast, then leaned back, wondering how a man as impatient as he seemed could do the kind of meticulous work he was known for. "You're not a very patient man, Cahill."

"I'm patient when I have time to be. Right now, we don't have time. You've got a case to solve. So do I. If eating wasn't a necessity, neither of us would be doing it."

"True."

"So, here's the thing, Jodie. I think you're the key to identifying Jane and John Doe. People here will open up to you. Ask the right questions, and you'll get the answers we need to put names and faces on our victims."

"Sorry to disappoint you, but I was an outsider when I lived here. I'm still an outsider. I just hope my presence doesn't make people even more closedmouthed than they were before I came."

The waitress set their food in front of them, and Jodie buttered a slice of toast, her stomach protesting at the thought of eating, the headache she'd had the night before back in full force.

"How can someone be an outsider in her hometown?"

"Not just my hometown. My home. Dad collects wives and ex-wives the way other people collect trinkets. He'd meet someone, date her, marry her, get tired of her and start all over again. Every time I got used to the house being one way, it changed. New décor, new rules." She shrugged, her cheeks heating. She'd said too much. This wasn't social hour, and Harrison wasn't a date. Even if he had been, she wouldn't have revealed so much about herself.

"Sounds like you had a rough childhood." He dug into his eggs, seeming to be completely relaxed and unconcerned with her reply. He wasn't. She could see the slight tension around his mouth, the sharpness behind his eyes. He wasn't just asking her about her childhood, he was trying to get information that he hoped would lead to the identity of John Doe. He could keep trying. She'd told him everything she knew.

"My story is no worse than most and better than many." She tore strips of crust from the bread, let the crumbs fall onto the plate. Hundreds of dark specks on white porcelain. How many times had she done the same when she was a kid, picking at food that had been served on heavy porcelain or delicate china, depending on the wife of the moment?

She pushed the plate away, wishing she'd never left headquarters. She'd wanted to escape Harrison and his questions.

All she'd succeeded in doing was dwelling on the past she had no liking for.

"What about you, Harrison? Did you have a *Father Knows Best* childhood? Mother baking cookies and Dad bringing home the money?"

He finished off his eggs, swallowed down some juice and stood. "I think our twenty minutes is up."

"I think you're avoiding my question."

"Everyone has secrets, Jodie. Even me." He smiled, but the darkness behind his eyes hinted at things Jodie hadn't expected. Sorrow. Pain. Harrison came off as confident and happy. She'd been sure he'd lived the kind of life she'd only dreamed of. Apparently, he hadn't. As much as she told herself she shouldn't be curious, she couldn't help wondering what had happened to make him the man he'd become—a man who seemed as dedicated to his job as she was to hers.

He waved the waitress over and paid the bill, refusing the money Jodie pulled from her wallet.

She shoved the bills into his hand and stood. "Take the cash, Cahill. It's not like we're on a date."

"A date? You're young enough to be my daughter. And I always pay when I'm interviewing witnesses."

"I'm not a witness, and you seem to have a real hang-up with my age."

"I'm just pointing out that there's a huge age difference between us."

"Huge? How old are you? One hundred?

"Thirty-eight."

"Ten years is not a huge age difference." A few years back, she'd dated a guy who was fifteen years her senior. The relationship had lasted as long as it took her to realize he thought she was young, naive and malleable, and for him to realize she wasn't.

"That's a matter of opinion." Harrison wasn't sure how

they'd gotten on the subject of age, dates and each other, but he was ready to get off it. He had a job to do in Loomis. He didn't have time for anything else. Or anyone.

He glanced at Jodie as they stepped outside, his stomach clenching as she met his eyes. Maybe *that* was why they'd gotten on the subject of dates and ages and each other. Every time he looked into her eyes, he forgot that she was an FBI agent, and a young one. He forgot that he didn't date women he worked with and that he'd given up on the idea of marriage and family. He forgot everything but the sadness he saw in her eyes. Sadness that made him want to pull her into his arms and tell her everything would be okay.

He doubted she'd appreciate the sentiment. Jodie's eyes might be sad, but the rest of her was as tough as nails.

"Jodie Gilmore! As I live and breathe! What are you doing back in town?" A voice called from the direction of the street, and Harrison scanned a line of cars waiting at a stoplight. A dark sedan idled near the curb, an older woman looking out the back window.

"Looks like you're about to get your chance to ask Charla Renault about that Swiss watch. Come on, I'll introduce you." Jodie's words were barely audible, but she gestured for him to follow, then turned and marched across the parking lot to introduce him to the woman he hoped would be able to help him put a name and a face to John Doe.

NINE

Jodie would have recognized Charla Renault anywhere. Ten years hadn't softened the hardness in her eyes or eased the tightness around her mouth. Bitterness aged as nothing else could, and Charla was definitely bitter.

"Mrs. Renault, it's good to see you again." She approached the car, knowing that Charla would make the final decision about whether the conversation would continue. The older woman had always had definite ideas about who fit into her social circle and who did not. As the child of a Pershing, Jodie never had before.

"I'm surprised you even remember who I am. You've been gone ten years." The tone made it an accusation, but then, almost everything Charla had ever said to Jodie sounded like an accusation.

"And now I'm back."

"A big shot FBI agent."

"Not a big shot, but I do work for the FBI."

"It's not a very feminine job, Jodie. You realize that, don't you?" Charla frowned, her gaze darting to Harrison before settling on Jodie again.

"I never thought about it one way or another."

"You should. If you ever want to find a husband, you need

to consider how you are perceived. Men don't like hard, tough women."

And yet somehow Charla had managed to marry and have children.

"I don't think any man would perceive Jodie as tough or hard, Mrs. Renault," Harrison cut in, standing up for Jodie in a way no one else ever had. His words warmed her, seeping into her soul and melting some of the ice that had formed there long ago.

"Do I know you, young man?" Charla frowned again, her dark eyes spearing Harrison with a look she had probably perfected long before Jodie had been born.

"We haven't met. I'm Harrison Cahill. A forensic anthropologist working for the FBI."

"Forensic anthropologist? How exciting!" Charla leaned a little farther out her window, her hair showing not a hint of gray even in the bright morning sunlight. A Jack Russel terrier hopped into her lap, and she stroked the small dog's fur.

"I'm not sure how exciting it actually is." Harrison offered a warm, lazy smile that made Jodie's heart flip and her pulse race.

"I've seen entire television shows dedicated to your profession, Mr. Cahill. Why, just a few nights ago, I watched a forensic anthropologist create a sculpted face from nothing but a skull. Fascinating." Charla was pouring on the charm, something Jodie had never seen her do before.

"That's part of what we do, Mrs. Renault, but only a small part. Another part of what we do is gather evidence. I was hoping you could help me do that."

"Really? How?"

"Perhaps you heard that we discovered two bodies near the swamp?"

Charla's eyes widened, her powdery skin going so pale that the blush on her cheeks stuck out in stark contrast. "Two bodies? That can't be."

"I'm afraid it can. They were found while the police were searching for a woman who's been missing for a couple of months. I'm sure you've heard about her disappearance." If Harrison felt guilty for upsetting Charla, he didn't look it.

"Who hasn't?" Charla's voice had lost some of its strength. "Whose bodies were found?"

"That hasn't been determined yet." Harrison glanced at Jodie, and she knew what he was thinking—that they had a pretty good idea about the identity of one victim.

"Then what is it you think I can do to help you?"

"One of the victims was wearing a watch. Gold. Good quality Swiss. An older model. From the eighties. Windup. With day and month display on it. The sheriff thought that if the victim was someone from Loomis, you might remember seeing the watch."

Charla didn't even think about it, just shook her head and sat back against her seat, apparently exhausted by the conversation. "I don't know anyone who has a watch like that."

"It wouldn't have been something you'd seen recently." Harrison tried again, his tone relaxed, as if he had all the time in the world to get the answers he wanted. The impatient energy Jodie had noticed earlier was gone, replaced by the slow meticulous nature she'd noticed at the crime scene.

"How long ago, Mr. Cahill? Months? Years?"

"Decades."

This time Charla looked as if she was thinking about it, going back through time, searching her memory. "You know, now that you mention it, I do recall someone at church having a very expensive watch. I remember thinking it was a frivolity. That the money would have been better spent on something else. Missions. Charity."

"Who did it belong to?" Jodie asked the question this time, her heart hammering with anticipation.

"I wish I could tell you, but aside from remembering what I thought about the watch, my mind is completely blank. I do know it's been a long time since I've seen it." Charla shrugged, her dark eyes flashing with impatience. "That's the problem with getting older—you forget more than you remember."

"The fact that you remembered the watch is great, Mrs. Renault. If you remember anything else, let the sheriff know, and he'll contact me." Harrison didn't seem disappointed by the lack of information and appeared content to take Charla at her word.

Jodie, on the other hand, wanted to ask how someone could remember a watch and not a person. She bit her lip and kept silent. There were other, more important questions she needed answers to. Annoying Charla wasn't the way to go about getting them.

"I'll do that, Mr. Cahill." Charla smiled at Harrison, then turned her attention back to Jodie. "Are you staying with your father, Jodie?"

"Yes."

"Well then, I'm sure I'll be seeing you at church Sunday."

"I…" What could she say? That she hadn't been to church in several months? That she had no desire to be in the same building with the people who had made her childhood miserable? "Maybe."

"Maybe? My dear, you really *must* attend. The new pastor is wonderful."

"I'm sure he is."

"He gave the eulogy at my son's funeral." Charla's voice broke.

"I was sorry to hear about Dylan's death."

"Everyone says that, but no one but a mother could understand the heartbreak my son's death has brought me."

"It must have been quite a shock. Dylan was always so well liked in the community." It wasn't really the truth. Dylan had been a player, a man who couldn't be trusted. Charming enough on the outside but not much worthwhile inside.

"Yes. It was a shock. So…brutal."

"A very personal crime."

"Yes."

"Do you think that someone Dylan knew could have been angry enough to—"

"There is no way it was someone Dylan knew. A stranger killed him. That is the only possible explanation." Charla took a handkerchief from her purse, dabbed at eyes that were bone-dry.

"Mrs. Renault, we never want to believe that someone we know could commit an unthinkable crime, but statistics show that murder victims most often know their murderer." Jodie tried to keep her voice gentle, but Charla's lack of tears bothered her. Why pretend to cry?

"You people have already investigated everyone Dylan knew. You even arrested that woman's worthless son." That woman was Charla's longtime rival, Lenore Pershing.

"We also released him. Since then, we haven't been able to find enough evidence to lead to an arrest. Maybe Dylan had an argument with someone, owed someone money."

"You're not implying that my son was killed because he was involved in something illegal."

"Of course not. I just don't want to close off any possibilities. We want to find his murderer, Mrs. Renault. No matter how difficult the questions are, they've got to be asked if we're going to do that. There were several other crimes committed since Leah Farley's disappearance. It's possible they are all related."

"My son's death was not related to Leah's disappearance nor was it connected to that Angelina woman's death." Charla huffed the words, and Jodie decided not to point out that Angelina and Dylan had been murdered with the same weapon.

"Do you think that Leah Farley willingly left Loomis? Is it possible that your son saw something happen to her?"

"I've answered these same questions a hundred times before." She let her head drop back against the seat, showing off her thin neck, encircled by several strands of pearls. There were pearl earrings in her ears. Tasteful. Expensive. Just like Charla.

"I—"

"You did hear about my accident five years ago, didn't you? My poor husband didn't survive it, and I've been unable to walk since. My strength and my health have just never been the same, have they. Bosworth?" Charla waved a hand at the car's driver, who shook his head in agreement.

"No. I hadn't heard. I'm sorry."

"These past few years have been so difficult. So difficult. Really, I'm exhausted. I simply must go home and rest."

The window rolled up then, and the car pulled away from the curb.

"Interesting lady." Harrison spoke quietly, and Jodie turned to face him.

"You're going to meet a lot of interesting people in Loomis."

"I already have."

"Aside from Charla, I mean."

"So do I." He smiled, the same charming smile he'd sent Charla's way, and Jodie's heart had the nerve to jump again.

"Don't waste your charm on me, Cahill. I'm immune."

"To me? Or to charm in general?"

"Both."

"Good to know." He cupped her elbow in his hand and walked toward her car. "I guess we'd better get back to headquarters. My case isn't solving itself."

"Neither is mine."

"You were questioning Charla about her son's murder. Sam mentioned yesterday that there had been two murders that matched the MO of the victims I'm trying to identify."

"Right. The woman Charla mentioned? She was murdered

in the same way, hit over the head and shot. Her body was found in the bayou. According to the file, she had a number of boy-friends and had been accused of blackmailing a few of them."

"Seems like a lot of crime for such a small town."

"There's more. Earl Farley, the husband of Leah Farley, the woman who is missing, was murdered, too. Different MO, though. His death was made to look like a suicide." They got in the car and she put it in gear, trying to ignore the masculine scent that suddenly filled her nose. Warmth. Comfort. Strength. Those were the things it reminded her of. Things she didn't need or want from anyone. Especially not Harrison.

"His wife's doing?"

"That's what we're trying to find out." There was a colored flyer on her car windshield; Jodie unrolled her window and reached around to pull it off, skimming the announcement, her muscles tensing as she read it.

Do you know a special mother? Nominate her to be this year's SanctiMommy. Then join us as we announce the winner at our twenty-fifth annual Mother of the Year awards!

Twenty-five years.

The first pageant had taken place on Mother's Day the year after Jodie's mother had left, and each one had been a painful reminder of what Jodie didn't have. She'd had usually spent Mother's Day holed up in her room avoiding anything and everything that had to do with the pageant.

"What is it?" Harrison's arm pressed against hers as he read the paper, his warmth seeping into her, begging her to lean into him, to let down her guard and tell him what she didn't even want to admit to herself. That the flyer was a reminder of what she'd hated most about Loomis—its fixation on motherhood, its yearly pageant that celebrated what Jodie had never had and what she knew she would never be.

"Nothing." She crumpled the paper tossed it into the backseat and drove to headquarters.

TEN

Sam Pierce was already at headquarters when they arrived, his dark head bent over a file folder. He looked up as she walked toward him, a frown carving lines at the sides of his mouth and creating shadows in the depth of his eyes. "I was wondering when you'd get here."

"I was talking to Charla Renault."

"Get any new information from her?"

"Other than the fact that she cries with dry eyes? Nothing."

"She cried real tears at her son's funeral. Maybe she's all cried out."

"Maybe. What have you got there? Anything interesting?" She gestured to the paper he'd been reading and dropped her purse onto a chair, determined to put her melancholy mood behind her.

"Actually, there is. Harrison, come on over and take a look. You might be interested in this, too. The bullets we found yesterday were from the same gun, but the weapon wasn't a match to the one used to kill Dylan Renault and Angelina Loring."

"Same MO, different weapon. Sounds like either you've got a killer who uses whatever gun happens to be handy or you've got a copycat on your hands." Harrison leaned closer to Jodie as he glanced down at the paper Sam was holding out.

Heat raced along her nerves at the closeness and she stepped away, putting distance between them, knowing that Harrison would notice but not caring. "I don't know how it could be a copycat. The remains have been in the underground tunnel for decades. Who could possibly have known about them?"

"Anyone who happened to go into that tunnel." Harrison spoke almost absently, his fingers tapping a beat against the desk.

"Are you making any headway on identify Jane and John Doe, Harrison?"

Jodie tensed at Sam's question. She'd been trying hard to forget that the woman who'd been lying dead for twenty-five years might be her mother.

Harrison hadn't forgotten. He met Jodie's eyes, his gaze steady as he answered, "I've got a lead, but nothing firm yet."

"You planning to let me in on what that lead is?" Sam raised a dark eyebrow, glancing from Harrison to Jodie and back again.

"You know I don't work that way. As soon as I've got all my facts together, I'll let you know what I've found."

"This isn't like most of the cases we call you in on, Harrison. We've got multiple cases and multiple victims, which may or may not be connected. I need whatever information you've got as soon as you've got it. Anything else just doesn't work for me." Sam's tone was reasonable enough, but irritation flashed in his eyes, and Jodie knew that the two men were about to go head-to-head over the matter.

"I'm Harrison's lead," Jodie said into the silence, and both men turned toward her.

"What do you mean, *you're* his lead?" Sam frowned and ran a hand along his jaw, obviously confused by the turn of events and not liking it. Everything she'd seen of him told Jodie that he was used to being in charge and in control. Having things happen outside of his plans would not be a good thing.

"I recognized a bracelet Jane Doe was wearing. It was one

just like my mother used to have." There. The words were out, and not nearly as painful as she'd expected them to be. Maybe because they were abstract and vague, leaving the possibility open that the victim wasn't her mother.

"Are you saying the woman we found is your mother?" To his credit, Sam looked appalled at the thought, his dark eyes filled with compassion.

"I'm saying it could be. My mother left town twenty-five years ago. I haven't seen her since."

"That doesn't mean—"

"She had long blond hair like mine. And she was having an affair. That's why she left my father." Jodie cut him off, not wanting to hear all the reasons why Jane Doe wasn't Amelia Pershing Gilmore. She'd spent half the night going over them all, and there weren't nearly enough to give her hope.

"Jodie—"

"It was a long time ago, so I really don't need to hear how sorry you are. Whether she's my mother or not isn't going to affect our investigation, but knowing her identity may point us in the right direction as far as finding her killer." She tried to smile, hoping to take the sting out of her words. She didn't want to be rude, but she also didn't want to hear Sam's words of comfort.

"Which may or may not lead us to Dylan and Angelina's killer and to Leah Farley." Sam let the subject of her mother drop, and Jodie was glad.

Talking about it wouldn't change anything. She'd deal with the truth as soon as she knew it. Until then, she'd focus her energy on finding Leah Farley. "The one thing we know for sure is that the recent trouble in Loomis began with Earl Farley's death. Supposedly a suicide, but as soon as police started investigating, his wife, Leah, disappeared."

"Sounds pretty straightforward." Harrison's words echoed

the ones Jodie had spoken when she'd been handed the case, and she couldn't help smiling in his direction.

"Funny, I said the same exact thing."

"And I bet your boss told you not to jump to conclusions." Harrison returned the smile, searching her face as if making sure she really was as okay as she'd claimed.

"Those were his exact words."

"They were good ones. I learned pretty quickly that the assumptions I made colored my investigations and closed me off to the possibilities. Speaking of which, I've got an appointment with the coroner. I want to see if he'll let me send a sample for DNA testing. I'll be back later to swab you, Jodie. The sheriff has a kit at his office that I'll pick up before I come back here."

"That's fine."

"See you then. I'll keep you posted on my progress, Sam." Harrison offered a quick wave and walked outside. Without him, the room felt empty to Jodie, the life and energy gone from it.

That surprised her. If she'd had to say who was more charismatic—Sam or Harrison—she would have picked Sam. He had a way of looking at people that made them feel as if what they had to say was truly important. No doubt that was why so many of the women at the New Orleans office had gone into mourning when the rumor went around that he'd gotten engaged. Harrison, on the other hand, was almost too intense, his steady gaze seeming to see much deeper than Jodie was comfortable with. She should be glad Harrison was gone.

She *was* glad he was gone. And if she said it enough, she just might believe it.

"If you want me to have Miles pull you from the case, I will, Jodie. Under the circumstances, everyone would understand if you asked to be given another assignment." Sam broke into her thoughts, offering her an easy out that she knew she couldn't take.

"That won't be necessary." If she left now, Loomis would win. There was no way she'd allow that to happen.

"You're sure?"

"Of course."

"Good. I'm willing to let you pull out, but I'd rather you didn't." He took another sheet of paper from the folder he'd been holding. "I got the blood-test results on the sample from the shoe this morning, too. Seems that blood on Leah's shoe wasn't her husband's. DNA testing was inconclusive, but the blood type didn't match Earl's."

"You had them test for a match to Leah?"

"Not yet. That's our next step. We need a DNA sample. Can you call her brother, see if he's got a hairbrush of hers? Also ask about her blood type. Blood typing on the sample came up as B positive."

"I can do that. Anything else?" She jotted notes on a pad of paper she grabbed from her desk.

"I want you to go talk to Leah's friend Shelby Mason. She works at the public library here in town. She seemed pretty forthcoming, but a little intimidated. She might relax more with you."

"How about the little girl? Sarah? Is there any sense in my trying to speak to her?"

"Let's leave it for now. She's been put through enough, and Jocelyn feels that Sarah has given us all the information she can."

"Jocelyn?"

"My fiancée. She's a child psychologist."

So Jocelyn was the child psychologist who'd stolen him away from New Orleans. Jodie almost smiled at the thought. It was nice to see someone finding happiness. Remarkable, even that happiness had been found in Loomis.

"That's fine. I'll call Leah's brother, then call the librarian."

"Shelby is usually at the library this time of the morning. She does children's corner every Friday."

"I'll go there now, then."

"Thanks. I'm going to New Orleans to brief Miles on the case. He wants answers. I wish I had more for him."

"We'll get them. I'll see you when you get back." She headed outside into the bright sunlight, shuddering at the hint of bayou that clung to the air. The scent seeped into her soul, stole the warmth that had been there when Harrison had looked into her eyes, touched her arm, made her feel like she mattered.

If Jodie hadn't given up on God years ago, she'd beg Him to give her a quick solution to this case, but she had given up. When she'd most needed to feel that God was with her, she'd felt alone, church services only reminding her of just how broken and sinful she was.

The sins of the father.

How many times had she heard the subject preached on? Each time, Jodie had left church feeling hopeless, destined to be exactly what she didn't want to be. But she hadn't become that. Despite her sinful mother, her troubled past, she had made something of herself. That was all she needed. All she wanted.

Wasn't it?

Sometimes she thought it wasn't. Sometimes she longed to believe that God was really there somewhere. Watching her, waiting for her to realize that the words she'd heard, the way she'd been treated, were nothing to do with Him and everything to do with the sins of others.

She pressed a hand against her temple, willing her headache away and willing away the longing that filled her. A longing she'd thought she'd let go of long ago.

The Loomis Library was just a few miles away from headquarters, and Jodie pulled into the back lot, checking her makeup in the rearview mirror. She looked too pale, the skin beneath her eyes bruised with fatigue, her lips pale pink and dry-looking. A little lip gloss, a dusting of blush and she was ready to step into the past.

Things hadn't changed much since the last time she'd walked through the library doors. The musty smell of old books mixed with the scent of furniture polish and copy-machine ink. A few people were seated in comfortable chairs, reading books or looking at newspapers. Several looked up as Jodie walked in, but she didn't acknowledge them. She was there to speak with Leah's friend. That was what she planned to do.

Jodie walked through the building, headed for the children's section. She was sure she remembered a Shelby. In high school, she'd been a little overweight with red hair and pretty features. Quiet and kind but not someone Jodie had ever spoken to. The only adult in the children's section was a redhead standing with her back to Jodie. Not at all overweight, she might have been Shelby or someone else entirely.

"Shelby Mason?" She spoke quietly, but the woman jumped anyway, spinning in her direction.

"Yes?"

"I'm sorry. I didn't mean to startle you. I'm FBI Agent Jodie Gilmore. I'm working to find your friend Leah Farley." She flashed her badge and a smile, hoping to put Shelby at ease.

"Jodie. You were a year behind me in school, weren't you?" Shelby smiled.

"I think so."

"I heard you were back in town. How have you been?"

"Fine." *Were they supposed to make small talk now?* Jodie had never been much for it, but she'd try if it would put Shelby at ease. "How about you?"

"I'll be better once we find Leah."

"You haven't heard anything from her since she left? No phone calls? E-mails? Text messages?"

"Nothing, and that's just not like Leah. Not only did she call me nearly every day, but also she'd never have left her daughter for more than a few hours without checking in."

"Sometimes people act out of desperation. Was there something going on in her life that might have made her feel like she needed to leave?"

Shelby cocked her head to one side, her long red hair sliding over her shoulder as she stared off into space, perhaps searching through vague memories and hoping for some hint of what might have happened to her friend. Finally, she sighed and shook her head. "No. I wish there was. At least then we'd have some idea of what happened."

"Her marriage to Earl was good?"

"Leah was doing her best to make things work."

"That's not an answer, Shelby." Jodie pulled out a notepad and began writing. This wasn't the first time she'd heard that Leah's marriage hadn't been all roses and love songs.

"Look, I don't want to cause trouble for Leah."

"How could you if she did nothing wrong?"

"She *didn't* do anything wrong, but Earl wasn't always the nicest guy in the world. There was some tension in their marriage. I think there were even times when she thought about divorce, but she never would have...killed him."

"Who would have?" Jodie looked up from the pad, watching Shelby's face, trying to read the truth in it. If Shelby knew anything, her expression didn't show it. She looked confused, worried, but not as if she was hiding something.

"I don't know, Jodie. I just know it wasn't Leah. She was a good person. A great mother. A strong Christian. She never would have committed murder."

"I believe that you believe that."

Shelby frowned. "She *didn't* do it."

"Then we need to find the evidence to prove it. If you hear from her, you need to tell her that she's got to come home. Aside from the fact that her daughter needs her, she's got a lot of questions that she needs to answer."

"I'll tell her." She glanced over as several children walked into the area. "That's my reading group. I've got to go. Let me know if there is anything else I do to help."

"I will. Thanks." Jodie moved back through the library, ignoring the stares of several library patrons. Some of the faces were familiar. None were people she was interested in speaking to, and she was tempted to walk out of the library and return to headquarters. At least when she was there, she wasn't under constant scrutiny.

She ignored the idea. There were things she could do at the library besides getting information from Shelby, and she was going to do them. The Mother of the Year Pageant flyer she'd seen earlier in the day had sparked a vague memory about a young mother's death. She couldn't remember the details, but she did know it had happened twenty-five years ago and had been the reason the pageant had been created.

Twenty-five years. Exactly the amount of time Jodie's mother had been missing.

If a woman *had* died in Loomis that same year, there'd be a newspaper article about it. Jodie needed to find it. She rubbed the back of her neck, trying to ease her tension and will some energy into her steps as she approached the information desk. The last thing she wanted was everyone in Loomis discussing how worn down and tired she looked. How harried and unable to cope. A failure. Just like they'd predicted. Like her father had predicted.

She straightened her spine and forced a pleasant smile as she approached the library's information desk. The librarian was happy to help Jodie find the information she wanted. Within minutes, she had Jodie seated in front of a computer, scrolling through archived newspapers that had been scanned into the database. At first, Jodie came up empty and was sure she'd be heading back to headquarters with nothing. Then bold, black letters jumped out at her, and she leaned forward, excitement racing through her blood and chasing away her fatigue.

Woman's Body Found at Gazebo.

By Roberta Pierce

LOOMIS—Yesterday morning, a man out jogging discovered a woman lying facedown on Loomis's community gazebo floor. Police, responding to the man's call for help, found the woman bleeding from a wound to the head and unresponsive. She was transferred to Loomis Hospital where she later was pronounced dead. Police have classified her death as suspicious and are investigating.

The article dated June 9th, gave the woman's name—Mary Sampson—and mentioned that she'd been happily married, the mother of one. Well liked. Admired. All the things that were usually said in the days following a death. The truth might be something quite different, but Jodie wasn't interested in that as much as in the crime itself. The woman had died of blunt force trauma to the head, but that was all that was said about her death. Police had never named a suspect. It had taken more than a month, but eventually Mary's murder ceased to be newsworthy.

And while her death was dissected and talked about, discussed and speculated on, two people had lain undiscovered, their brutal murders a dark secret that only one person knew.

ELEVEN

Jodie knew what she had to do, but she wasn't happy about it. She needed the police report and case file. She needed to check the MO of the crime, find out if there could be a match between it and the other two murders that had happened within days of the attack.

Getting the file meant going to the Sheriff's department and asking Sheriff Reed to allow her access to it. He wouldn't give it willingly. She knew that before she even made the drive to his office. She also knew she could ask Sam to get the file for her. He'd do it, and he probably wouldn't think any less of her because she'd asked.

Jodie, on the other hand, would think a whole lot less of herself. The Sheriff's office was just off Main Street, and Jodie pulled into a metered parking space in front of the building, telling herself she had every right to be there. Like any other FBI agent, she had the responsibility and the authority that went with her job.

If she could just keep that in mind, she'd be fine.

She took a deep breath and stepped out into the warm spring day. The trees were alive with color, their bright green leaves and vivid pink blossoms a striking contrast to the azure sky. In any other town, Jodie would have found the beauty of the scene enthralling, but in Loomis she could see it only as a coat of paint hiding the ugliness beneath.

A young freckle-faced desk sergeant looked up as Jodie entered the building. "Can I help you, ma'am?"

Ma'am? Did she look that old? "I'd like to speak with Sheriff Reed."

"Is he expecting you?"

"No. My name is Jodie Gilmore. I'm—"

The kid's eyes widened and he straightened in his seat. "The Jodie Gilmore who ran off when she was eighteen and came back as an FBI agent?"

"That's right."

"Everyone at Loomis University is talking about you. There isn't a person there who doesn't wish he had the guts to do what you did."

Guts? It hadn't been guts that sent her running. It had been cowardice.

"It's never too late to go after your dreams." It was an inane platitude, but the deputy didn't seem to mind.

"You're right, but it sure is difficult to change direction once you've headed a certain way."

"You want to pursue a career with the FBI?"

"Honestly, I don't know. I just know I don't want to spend the rest of my life in this little town. But don't tell Sheriff Reed I said that. He's not so hot on big-city cops. Says they don't know squat about police work." He smiled sheepishly.

"Your secret is safe with me."

"Good. Tell you what, the sheriff is eating lunch. Why don't I just go back and see if he has a minute to speak with you?"

"Thank you, Deputy…?"

"Franklin. William Franklin." He shot out of his chair and disappeared through an open doorway.

Jodie paced the small waiting area, wishing she really were

the gutsy heroic figure the Loomis University students seemed to think she was. There'd been times in her life when she'd wondered what would have happened if she'd had the courage to stay in Loomis, but most of the time she knew she'd done what she had to.

Sheriff Reed stepped through the open doorway and scowled in Jodie's direction. "I'd have thought your father would have taught you better manners than to show up unannounced and uninvited."

"This isn't a social call, Sheriff. I don't think I need to play by the rules of etiquette."

"Would have been nice if you had, is all I'm saying. Come on back to my office. I don't have a lot of time, so I'm going to have to eat while we talk." He turned on his heel and walked away before Jodie could protest.

Jodie followed, feeling like a kid going to the principal's office and frustrated with herself because of it. She had the upper hand here. Not the other way around. She needed to keep that in mind or Reed would walk all over her.

Sheriff Reed's office was large and airy, the windows letting in enough light to give it a cheerful look.

Cheerful was the last thing Jodie felt as she settled into a chair across the desk from the sheriff.

She put on her best FBI manners anyway. It would do no good to annoy the sheriff. "Thank you for giving me a few minutes of your time."

"It's not a problem. We do go way back, after all. So, you want to tell me what was so important you had to interrupt my lunch?" He bit into an overstuffed sandwich, his puffy fingers looking like pale sausages against the dark rye bread.

"I'm curious about a murder that happened here twenty-five years ago. A woman named Mary Sampson. She was found dead at the gazebo."

"Think you have to fill me in on the details? That was one of my first cases. I was a deputy then. Young and green. Got one look at the blood under her head and puked up my dinner." He steepled his fingers under his chin and stared at Jodie, searching her face with a casual arrogance she found irritating.

"She was killed by blunt-force trauma to the head, right?"

"Yep. Two blows to the head. One to the front. The other to the back. Looked like she'd been hit, tried to crawl or run away and was hit again."

"And you never found her murderer?"

"Nope. Didn't even have enough evidence to point a finger at someone. Why are you so interested in something that happened when you were a baby?"

"I was three, actually. And I'm interested because Mary was killed in June."

"Yeah? So?" He took another bite of his sandwich and wiped a napkin across his mouth.

"So that's when our Jane and John Doe were murdered. It seems like a stretch to think that's a coincidence."

"All three killed the same month? Does seem a little odd."

A little odd wasn't Jodie's word for it, but she kept silent, hoping the sheriff would keep talking. He didn't disappoint her.

"You know, Mary's murder and your mother leaving happened within days of each other. People in town were talking about curses and the like. Two young mothers suddenly gone. One violently murdered. The other just taking off and leaving her kid. Seemed unnatural, you know?" He shook his head, grabbed a bottle of soda from beside his desk. "You want one? I've got a couple more of these."

"No, thanks."

"So, you're thinking you may have a serial killer. Is that it? That whoever murdered Mary also murdered the two people in that tunnel?" He popped a potato chip into his mouth and eyed her with a cold, hard stare.

"At the moment, I'm collecting evidence. I'd like to see Mary Sampson's file."

"It's downstairs in the storage area. Don't know exactly where, but I can tell you for sure, *I'm* not going down there to get it."

A soft knock sounded on the door, and the deputy peeked in. "Sheriff? You've got another visitor."

"What is this? Grand Central Station?" Reed crumpled a brown paper bag and tossed it into a trash can. "Who is it this time?"

"A guy who says he's working for the FBI. Harrison Cahill."

Harrison was here? Just his name made Jodie's cheeks heat and her pulse race. Stupid. Childish.

Completely out of her control.

"Tell him he'll have to come back later. I can only deal with one problem at a time." He emphasized the word *problem,* his irritated gaze never leaving Jodie's face.

"I tried, but—"

"Cahill didn't have time to play games, so he came back anyway." Harrison spoke as he stepped into the room, his eyes the same green as new spring grass, his dress shirt unbuttoned at the collar. Hair slightly ruffled, tie hanging loose around his neck, he looked like a young Indiana Jones. So compelling Jodie had to tear her gaze away.

"You're going to have to come back another time, Cahill. I've got to help the FBI agent before I can help you." Sheriff Reed stood and stretched, his belly straining against the confines of his shirt.

"I came for the DNA kit you said you had. I'm sure it won't be too much trouble to find it."

"Won't be too much trouble to find after I deal with Jodie."

"You don't have to *deal* with me, Sheriff. You've got to give me the file I need. Then I'll be out of your hair." Jodie stood too, refusing to allow the two men to tower over her.

"You've both got the patience of two-year-olds." Reed lifted a set of keys from his desk and tossed them to Jodie. "Those are to the storage area downstairs. Mary's file is in one of the boxes labeled with the year of her murder. Shouldn't be too hard to find."

"Thanks." She scooted past Harrison, careful not to brush against him as she moved. She felt his presence anyway, filling the room, pulling her in.

"I'll come help while the sheriff finds that DNA kit."

"I'm fine, Cahill. Thanks for the offer, though."

"You're fine." He stepped out into the hall and closed the sheriff's door, then leaned close to her ear, his breath whispering against her skin, as soft as a butterfly's wings. "But I'm not. If I do what I want and deck the sheriff, I'll be thrown in jail faster than you can say, 'justifiable homicide.'"

"Justifiable homicide? You might just get away with it."

"Maybe, but the trial would take too much time away from my work, and I'm already behind. Come on, I think the stairs are this way." He grabbed her shoulder and gently pushed her forward, his touch more familiar than it should have been.

"Are you always this touchy-feely?" She frowned, pulling away.

"Not that I'm aware of. I guess you just bring out the best in me." He grinned and pushed open a door that led into a narrow stairwell.

"Well, if you don't stop it, you're going to bring out the worst in me." She mumbled the words as they started down a flight of steep steps, but he heard.

"Promises, promises." He moved quickly, taking the uneven cement stairs two at a time.

"Slow down, Cahill. These steps are hazardous." Jodie moved more slowly, her low-heeled pumps making the stairs even more difficult to navigate.

"Don't worry. If you fall, I'll catch you."

"The last person who told me that decided he'd rather run than break his back. He made it home in one piece. I broke my arm and ended up being grounded for a month."

"You were grounded for breaking your arm?"

"I was grounded for trespassing."

"Trespassing?" He waited at the bottom of the stairs, watching as she walked down, his shoulders relaxed, his expression unreadable. He might have been interested in hearing the story or not, but Jodie had the feeling he was. She also had the feeling it would be a mistake to share more of herself with him.

For reasons she couldn't explain, she told the story anyway, spinning what had been a horrifying experience into a humorous tale. "A friend dared me to go into an abandoned house at the edge of town. I was supposed to run upstairs and look out the back window to prove I'd done it. A neighbor must have called the police, because I was hanging out the back window waving when we heard sirens. My friend said I'd never make it downstairs and outside before the police got there. He said if I jumped he'd catch me, and we'd both run home before anyone ever knew we were there."

"And you listened?"

"I was ten. He was twelve and cute." She stepped off the last stair. "I jumped just as a police officer came around the side of the house. My friend ran. I fell. Next thing I knew, I was in the hospital, my father's wife pacing the floor and griping about missing her hair appointment."

"Nice story, Gilmore."

"You asked." She smiled, glancing around the cavernous basement until she found the room she was looking for. "That's the storage room. Hopefully, the file will be where it's supposed to be."

She started across the room, but Harrison put a hand on her

shoulder, pulling her to a stop. "For the record, Gilmore, I'd never run and leave you behind."

"For the record, I've outgrown crushes, and my days of jumping when someone tells me to are over."

"Good to know if we ever get trapped on the second floor of a burning building." A half smile softened the hard line of his jaw and deepened the green of his eyes but did nothing to ease his intensity.

If she looked long enough, if she allowed herself to, Jodie knew she'd see more than she wanted to. Attraction. Interest. But men were trouble. Way too much trouble. She needed to remember that when she was around Harrison. If she didn't, she might find herself on the wrong side of a second-story window, getting ready to jump again. And despite his promise, Jodie had no real hope that Harrison would be there to catch her.

TWELVE

Harrison wasn't quite sure what he was doing in the basement of the Loomis Sheriff's department with Jodie. When he'd seen her car parked in front of the building, he'd almost driven by. Waiting a few more hours to get the DNA kit wouldn't have hurt, and staying away from a woman he shouldn't be interested in seemed like a good idea.

He'd parked his car anyway and gone inside.

He told himself he was curious to know what Jodie was doing there. The truth was, he was curious to know more about her. Who was she, really? What other secrets was she hiding?

If there was more to his interest, Harrison refused to admit it. The way he saw it, if God wanted him married with kids, things would have worked out with Allison.

"I hope the file is easy to find. I've got a half-dozen other things I need to accomplish today." Jodie's tone revealed none of what she was feeling, but Harrison didn't miss the tightness of her movements as she unlocked the door.

He made her uncomfortable.

Good. She made him uncomfortable, too. Since his breakup with Allison, he'd been on a few dates, but none of the women he'd been out with had stuck in his mind, made him want to spend more time with them, know more about them. He hadn't wanted to look into their eyes and keep looking until every question was answered, every secret known.

He frowned, leaning a shoulder against the wall as Jodie stepped into the room. She was ten years younger than he was. That was about five years younger than anyone he'd ever been interested in. He'd better keep that in mind before he ended up involved in a lot more than a murder investigation. He shook his head to clear it, then turned to Jodie.

"Add one more thing to the list. You need to let me get that DNA sample from you."

"That'll take all of two seconds."

"What are we looking for?"

"*I'm* looking for an unsolved murder case file."

"Give me the name. I'll help you find it."

"Mary Sampson."

"Looks like everything is filed by date and name. When did the murder take place?" He scanned a stack of boxes against one wall.

"Twenty-five years ago."

"Twenty-five years seems to be a theme around Loomis."

"That, and the month of June. Mary was found bleeding on the floor of the gazebo on the ninth of June. She died at Loomis Hospital shortly thereafter. You said our victims were murdered sometime around the eleventh."

"And that's why we're down here, searching through old case files?"

"I want to know exactly how she was killed. The newspaper gave limited information. Not enough to see if we've got a matching MO." She seemed more relaxed than she had been, her blond hair sliding over her shoulder as she leaned down to look through a box of files.

Harrison knelt down and pulled a couple of boxes away from the wall. Something flowery and feminine hung in the air, mixing with the musty scent of dust and moisture. "It's possible you're looking at the work of a serial killer."

"If so, let's pray we find him before he kills anyone else." She shoved the box she'd been looking through away and pulled another one toward her. "This is it."

"The entire box?" Curious, Harrison studied the cardboard container. It had been sealed with tape and didn't look like it had been opened in years.

"Looks that way. With any luck, there will be some DNA evidence in here. Something we can use to match our crimes." Jodie pulled a penknife from her pocket and slit the tape.

"Let's hope none of it has been contaminated."

"Sheriff Reed wasn't in charge back then." She sounded distracted, her focus seeming to be only partially on the conversation.

Harrison couldn't blame her. He was the same way when faced with a new assignment or new evidence. He needed time to think it all through, formulate a plan, decide how best to move forward with the job.

"If we find forensic evidence that links this case with ours, we can start looking at common denominators. Maybe we'll find our murderer that way."

"Cahill, things are never that easy in Loomis." She glanced up from a sheaf of papers she'd lifted from the box, her eyes shadowed and dark, a soft smile hovering at the corners of her lips.

"They sure weren't for you, were they?" The question slipped out and Jodie stiffened, the softness he'd seen in her gone.

"I don't like to talk about my past, Cahill. It's something I prefer to forget."

"You can't forget something you're living in. Being in this town is like living in a time capsule. People around here don't seem to forget anything."

"You're right about that." Jodie turned her attention back to the papers. "This is all vague. The woman died of blunt-force trauma to the head. The coroner speculated that she'd been hit with a baseball bat, but no weapon was found."

"Was she sexually assaulted?"

"No. And her purse was found beside her body. Credit cards and money still inside. Her wedding and engagement rings were still on her finger. It wasn't a robbery." She shrugged, her cotton shirt pulling against her shoulders.

She was thin Harrison noticed. Too thin. She'd barely eaten anything that morning. Had she eaten lunch?

Why was he worrying about it? He'd decided after Allison, that God had plans for his life that didn't include marriage. He forced his thoughts back to the case.

"Any possible motives?"

"Not according to the report. Her husband adored her. She didn't stick her nose into other people's business. Her neighbors respected her and didn't have a bad word to say about her."

"The husband might have been having an affair and decided he wanted out of the relationship but didn't want to share the kids." He'd seen the results of that scenario too many times during the course of his career.

"He was the only suspect, and—" she paused, flipped back through the pages "—he had an airtight alibi. He was with the army reserves and had training that weekend. He'd been gone since early that morning."

"It's easy enough to hire someone to commit murder." Another thing he'd seen before.

"There were no large sums of money withdrawn from the account. There was no life insurance on the wife. According to this report, the husband was distraught. Whether or not he was putting on an act, I don't know."

"What else is in the box?"

"Looks like the woman's shirt." She lifted a sealed plastic bag. "Blood splatter on the collar and shoulder. Looks like there's more other places, but I can't see it all."

"She must have been hit hard."

"A man, then. Or a very strong, very angry woman."

"Maybe Mary was the one having an affair?"

"Anything is possible." She set the shirt back in the box and lifted another plastic bag. "This is interesting."

"What?" He leaned in, inhaling sunshine and flowers.

"It's a camera. She must have had it with her." She ran her finger down a page of the document. "There was no film in the camera when it was found."

Harrison took the bag from her hand and looked at the camera, his mind racing with possibilities. A Nikon. Good quality. Expensive. Not something an amateur photographer would buy. A zoom lens was attached, the glass cracked. "Was she into photography?"

"The report doesn't say."

"It could be she was down by the bayou, taking pictures. It could also be that she got a photograph of our murderer."

"I was thinking the same thing. She'd been at a women's auxiliary meeting that afternoon. Her kids were spending the night at a friend's house. According to newspaper reports, Mary's husband moved away a month after she was killed. I'll ask Sheriff Reed if he knows his current contact information." Jodie placed everything back in the box and closed it.

"I think the only thing Reed knows is the number of days until his retirement." Harrison stood and offered Jodie a hand up. Her palm was small and warm against his, her skin as soft as silk. Her hair would be the same, he imagined, and suddenly wanted to let the sleek length of it slide through his fingers.

Not a good thing to be imagining, especially when they were alone in a very small room in a very quiet basement. He released his hold and stepped away. "Speaking of Reed, I'd better go see if I can get him moving on that DNA kit."

"And I'd better get back to headquarters with the information I've got. I want to e-mail it to Sam. He's working in New Orleans today." She shoved the box with her foot, frowning a little. "Too bad I haven't found as much information about Leah Farley as I have about a murder that happened twenty-five years ago."

"How long has Leah Farley been missing?"

"Two months. We're not sure if she's met with foul play or if she's in hiding. If she's hiding, she's doing a good job of it. No paper trails. No phone calls. Nothing."

"You know what that means."

"I know what it probably means, but it's not the outcome we're hoping for." She stepped out of the storage room, waiting for him to exit, then closed and locked the door. "I hate to think of her daughter spending the rest of her life without a mother."

"Like you did?" There he went again, asking questions he had no right to.

"You keep bringing up my past, Cahill." She glanced over her shoulder as she started up the stairs, her eyes unreadable.

"I'm curious."

"Why?"

"I'd like to say that it's because understanding you will help me understand how things work around here, and that understanding that will help with my investigation."

"But you won't?"

"That would be a lie, and I don't make a habit of lying." He reached around Jodie and pushed open the door that led to the main corridor.

"You just make it a habit of asking questions about things that have nothing to do with you?"

"Who says it has nothing to do with me?"

"You did. If I remember correctly, you said I was young enough to be your daughter."

"And as you pointed out, that was a slight exaggeration."

"Slight?" She paused at the door to Sheriff Reed's office. "Cahill, I dated a man years older than you and he wasn't even close to being my father's age. At the time, I thought men my age were immature."

"At the time?"

"I was eighteen."

An eighteen-year-old Jodie with an older man? The thought made Harrison's muscles tense. "What was a guy that age doing with a teenager?"

"I was an adult, living on my own, working two jobs and going to college. He was trying to mold me into his idea of the perfect woman. I'm afraid I wasn't quite as malleable as he thought."

"And?"

"And I broke up with him about two months into the relationship, packed up my stuff, moved to a new town, got a couple of new jobs and enrolled in college." She shrugged as if it weren't a big deal, but Harrison knew it was.

"So you ran and wound up in Baltimore, where you ended up becoming a cop."

"You've got a good memory, Cahill, but I think we're both too busy to stand around talking anymore right now." She knocked on the door to the sheriff's office, pushing it open when the sheriff called for them to enter.

Reed was still sitting behind his desk, working on the complicated task of finishing off his bag of chips. "You all find what you were looking for?"

"Yes." Jodie dropped the key on his desk. "Do you remember much about Mary Sampson?"

"She worked freelance for the newspaper. Just wrote local interest stories. Nothing fancy."

"She had her camera with her when she died." Jodie ran a hand over her hair, hoping the impatience she felt wasn't in her voice. Sheriff Reed worked at his own pace. Trying to rush him was a waste of time.

"Yup. No film, though."

"Did anyone think that was odd?"

"Don't know. It wasn't my case." He leaned back, his hands behind his head, his dark eyes scanning her from head to toe. She didn't fidget under his scrutiny. She'd met more irritating men and more dangerous ones. Sheriff Reed was just a small bump in the road.

"I'm sure people talked about the case. It was in the newspaper for weeks."

"Looked that up, did you? You really are a big-time agent." His words held a hint of mockery, and she knew if Harrison hadn't walked in the room with her, there would have been more than that.

"I'm just doing my job, Sheriff." *Which is a lot more than you're doing.* She bit back the words, refusing to be less than professional.

"Thought you were here to find Leah Farley. Not dig into old cases."

"I'm here to find Leah, but her case is complicated and so is the investigation."

"Seems to me that maybe it's you people who are complicating things."

She ignored his comment, focusing on getting the information she wanted and getting out of his office. "Do you have any contact with Mary's husband?"

"Haven't heard from him in ten years or more."

"Do you know where he can be reached?"

"Nope."

"Do you have any idea—"

"You can keep asking me questions all day. I got no answers. The woman was murdered twenty-five years ago. Too long ago to be worried about it now."

"If she were your wife, mother or daughter, would you be saying that?" Harrison nearly growled the question, his disgust with the sheriff obvious. Apparently, he wasn't nearly as worried about being seen as a professional as Jodie was.

"None of the women in my family would be dumb enough to be outside late at night."

"So you're blaming the victim?" Harrison stepped farther into the room, nudging past Jodie.

She wasn't sure what he planned and put a hand on his shoulder, feeling firm muscles and warm flesh through his shirt. Heat shot up her arm at the contact, but she didn't release her hold. "Cool it, Cahill."

"Don't worry, Gilmore. I'm not going to do something that'll get me into trouble."

"Glad to hear it." She let her hand drop away. "I've got to go back to headquarters. Let me know when you get the DNA kit."

"Right. Did you find the kit, Sheriff?"

"Haven't had time yet. How about you go back to what you were doing and I'll call you once I find it."

"How about I just take a seat and wait until you have time?" Harrison dropped into the chair across from the sheriff, looking calm and in control.

Jodie bit back a smile.

She didn't know Harrison well, but she knew he'd sit there for as long as it took to get what he'd come for. Minutes. Hours. She was tempted to stick around just to see how long it would be before the sheriff realized that.

Tempted, but she wouldn't. She had things to do that didn't include watching a very handsome, very charming man rile Sheriff Bradford Reed.

"I'd better get back to headquarters."

Harrison snagged the back of her shirt before she could leave. "Do me a favor, will you?"

She turned, meeting his eyes, her breath catching as she stared into their deep green depth. "That depends on what it is."

"Stick around headquarters until I get back." He didn't say why. He didn't have to. The sooner they got the DNA samples in, the sooner they'd know whether Jane Doe was her mother.

"I can do that."

"Good. And maybe you could grab some lunch and bring it back here to share. I have a feeling Reed is going to be a while. We can eat together." His warm smile pulled her in, made her feel like she belonged, and Jodie took a step away, her heart hammering, her mind screaming that she'd better be careful.

"Sorry, I was an only child. I never learned to share." With that she walked out the door and hurried to her car, anxious to get back to work and forget about Harrison Cahill and his deep green eyes and charming smile.

THIRTEEN

Jodie returned to headquarters, e-mailed the information regarding Mary Sampson to Sam and then grabbed Leah Farley's file. Like Mary Sampson, Leah had been a loving mother, a good wife and a well-liked neighbor. A churchgoer who devoted herself to others, she seemed to be exactly what her friend Shelby had said she was—a law-abiding citizen, who wouldn't harm a soul and who would never abandon her daughter. Somehow, though, her husband had wound up with a bullet in the head and Leah had wound up missing.

Coincidence?

Of course not. The two things had to be related, but that didn't mean that Leah was a murderer. It also didn't mean she was dead. There were other explanations for her disappearance. They were just a lot less likely and a lot more difficult to come up with.

Jodie sighed and rubbed eyes that burned from fatigue. Her head still throbbed, her stomach was empty and she wanted desperately to drive out of town and never look back. There were so many more interesting places she could be. So many more *comfortable* places.

Her cell phone rang and she grabbed it, happy for the distraction. "Gilmore here."

"Jodie? It's Susan."

"Hi, Susan. What can I do for you?" Surprised, Jodie leaned back in her chair, staring up at the watermarked ceiling and wondering what her stepmother could possibly have to say. In the three years she'd been married to Richard, Susan had never called Jodie. Then again, Jodie had never called her.

"I was calling to let you know that we'll be having a formal dinner tonight in honor of your visit."

A formal dinner. That couldn't be good and wouldn't be pleasant. Jodie had no desire to sit in the cavernous dining room where she'd so often eaten breakfast and dinner alone, now making small talk with a father who hadn't had the time of day for her when she was a troubled kid. "Things are really hectic with the case I'm working on, Susan. I just don't think I'll be able to make it."

"But your father and I had plans to go to the movies tonight, and I told him that since you were in town, we really should have dinner to celebrate."

"Really, I—"

"I married late in life, Jodie. I never had children of my own, and I never will. Let me treat you like family while you're here."

How could she say no to that?

She couldn't. That's how. "I guess I can do dinner, but—"

"Wonderful! I've asked our chef to create something I know you'll enjoy. Your father wants you here at seven. Bring a friend if you can, to even out our numbers. See you then."

The line clicked and Susan was gone.

Come at seven. Bring a friend if you can?

At twenty-eight years old, Jodie was suddenly taking orders from a woman who wanted to play mother? She would have laughed if she weren't so frustrated. "I can't believe this."

"Believe what?" Deep and resonant, Harrison's voice drifted across the room and slid along Jodie's nerves, making her heart leap.

Foolish, fickle heart.

She frowned, swiveling in her chair to face him, her heart doing a little dance when she saw him a few feet away. Dark hair, strong features, eyes deep forest green. Too handsome. Too charming.

Too tempting.

Every time she looked in his eyes, she saw a glimpse of the dreams she thought she'd left far behind. "Next time warn a girl, Cahill. I didn't even hear you come in."

"You were too busy scowling at the phone. So? What can't you believe?"

"I can't believe that a woman I met less than twenty-four hours ago wants to pretend we're family."

"What woman?" He grabbed a chair and pulled it over, setting a plastic bag on the table next to Jodie.

"My stepmother." A rich, spicy aroma drifted from the bag, and Jodie's stomach growled. Loudly.

Harrison smiled, his eyes flashing with humor. "Hungry?"

"I haven't eaten lunch."

"I suppose I should point out that I asked you to bring lunch over to the sheriff's office for us to share."

"I was busy."

"So was I, but I managed to stop for food." He opened the plastic sack. "And unlike you, I had a sibling, so I know how to share."

Amused, Jodie took the wrapped sandwich he handed her. "I guess I should thank your parents for teaching you good manners."

"You'd have to thank my grandparents. My parents were killed when I was eleven. My grandparents became Mom and Dad after that."

"I'm sorry."

"It was rough. They were doing mission work in the Amazon when the plane they were in went down. There were ten people aboard. Only four of them were ever identified. My mother was, but not my father. My grandmother always wondered if he might be alive somewhere. I always wondered, too." He shook his head, pulling another sandwich out of the bag.

"Is that why you became a forensic anthropologist?"

"One of the reasons. Maybe the most important one. I enjoy what I do. The fact that I help people find closure after tragedies is a big part of what I love about it, but it isn't everything. There's the puzzle that needs solving, the sculpture that comes to life under my hands when I'm creating a likeness of the deceased." He placed his sandwich on the desk and grabbed Jodie's wrist before she could lift her sandwich to her mouth. "Hold on. We've got two things to do before we eat."

"What?"

"DNA swab first." He pulled out a DNA kit, opening it and taking out the swab. "Open up."

Jodie did as she was told, knowing it was the quickest way to confirm or deny whether the woman's remains belonged to her mother.

Remains.

What was left after the soul departed. An empty shell. Nothing to get worked up over, but Jodie's eyes burned with tears, and she turned away as soon as Harrison finished. "What else do we need to do?"

"Thank God for the food He's provided."

Was he serious? "Aren't we a little old for that?"

"Since when does a person get too old to say thank you?"

Her cheeks heated at his gentle chiding, and she took the hand he offered. "Go ahead."

He stared into her eyes for a minute, and Jodie was sure he

was going to ask if she was uncomfortable or say that he'd pray without her if she'd rather.

Instead, he squeezed her hand, then closed his eyes and prayed. The words were simple rather than flowery, gratitude as straightforward as Harrison was. When he finished, he lifted his sandwich and took a bite.

If he'd said something about Jodie's unwillingness to pray, she could have easily put him out of her mind and convinced her traitorous heart that he wasn't worthy of leaps and jumps and jigs.

Of course, he didn't.

"I'm overnighting the DNA sample I took from you along with a molar from the deceased. I think there should be enough DNA there to confirm or refute our belief that Jane Doe is your mother. My friend promised to expedite the testing. We should have it in a few days, tops."

He pulled chips from the bag and tossed a pack to Jodie. "Mitch owes me a favor. He'll work after hours to get the job done."

"I appreciate it."

"The sooner this case is closed, the sooner we can both get back to New Orleans."

"Have you already started the facial reconstruction?"

"Yeah, I went to the coroner's office before I visited our friend the sheriff. The coroner, by the way, is a lot more helpful than Reed. Tomorrow I'm going to start putting a face on our male victim. I've already got the skull scanned into my computer, and I'm going to do more prep work this afternoon."

"We can saturate local news with the face once you've got one for us."

"Give me another forty-eight hours. I—"

The door swung open, warm moist air blowing in on a soft spring breeze as Vera Peel swept in. Faded red hair scraped back into a tight bun, her long face pale, she scowled at Harrison. "Mr. Cahill, we need to talk."

"Do we?" Harrison stood, not seeming at all perturbed by Vera's obvious irritation.

"Yes. I went to clean the powder room this morning and the light was on. Do you know how much it costs to keep a place like mine running? With what your people are paying me to keep you, I can't afford a high electric bill."

"I'll certainly keep that in mind, Mrs. Peel." Harrison didn't even crack a smile. Which was more than Jodie could say for herself.

"Is something amusing you, Jodie?" Vera speared her with a cold gaze, and Jodie worked to school her features. If Vera spread rumors that Jodie didn't take her job seriously, it would be that much more difficult to get information from people.

"I guess I'm just surprised you'd come into town to talk to Harrison about a light in the powder room."

"I did not come specifically for that purpose. I came into town for the women's Bible study, which I need to be at in—" she glanced at her watch "—ten minutes. Since I was here anyway, I thought I would drop by and let Mr. Cahill know how I feel." Her cold gaze traveled the breadth and width of the room as if she were searching for something.

"Do you need something else, Mrs. Peel?" If not, Jodie was ready for the woman to leave. She might be harmless, but she'd always given Jodie the shivers.

"I heard you people pulled two bodies out of that tunnel out by the bayou. The one that was part of the Underground Railroad."

"Where did you hear that?"

"My friend's son is a deputy with the Loomis Sheriff's department. He was just full of news about it. Said that was why Mr. Cahill was here."

"It is. But if you're looking for the bodies, you won't find them here. They were transferred to the county coroner's office." Harrison didn't seem bothered by Vera's nosiness. Jodie was. She knew how quickly rumors could spread. If Vera decided to take the truth and twist it, any number of stories could be circulating by morning.

"As soon as we have more information, we'll be happy to share it, Mrs. Peel." Jodie hoped her comment would cut off further questions. She should have known better.

"Do you know who they were? The people who died, I mean?"

"Not yet."

"What did they look like? Someone around here probably knew them."

"They have been dead for at least two decades. There was no identification, so it will take some time to figure out who they were." Harrison finished his chips and tossed the empty bag in the trash can.

"You'd think that if someone was missing for that long we all would have heard about it. Maybe the people you found were homeless and using the house as a place to live. It's been abandoned for years, you know."

"It's possible." Harrison smiled and walked toward the door. "I know you've got a Bible study to attend, and I wouldn't want you to be late. How about I walk you to your car."

Vera blinked, her beady eyes shifting from Harrison to the desk where two half-eaten sandwiches sat side by side. "I see. You want me to leave because I've interrupted your tryst."

Jodie's cheeks flamed, but she refused to be cowed by the woman. "It's not a tryst, Mrs. Peel. Harrison and I were discussing the case over lunch."

"You expect me to believe that? You're the image of your mother, Jodie Gilmore. And obviously you're made of the same moral fiber." Vera pivoted and marched to the door, her back straight, her posture stiff as she walked outside.

"That woman is as creepy as her house." Harrison settled back down in the chair and took a bite out of his sandwich.

"She's been that way forever. There was some kind of story about her." Jodie remembered it vaguely. Something about a marriage that had gone wrong.

"It seems to me there is a story about everyone in this town."

"There is, and if you stay here long enough, you'll hear every one."

"But how much of what I'd hear would be the truth?"

"Good question. I don't have an answer to it. I don't even know if the story about my mother having an affair is true. I know one thing for sure, though—Vera believes it." She shrugged her shoulders, trying to ease the tension there.

"The woman is a few cards short of a full deck."

"That doesn't mean I enjoy the glares she shoots in my direction every time she sees me." She finished her sandwich, brushed crumbs from the desk and stood. "I need to get back to work. Thanks for the sandwich."

"Is that my cue to leave?"

"You said you were going back to the coroner's office. I don't want to keep you from your work. Besides, I'm having dinner with my father and stepmother. I need to finish my own work before then."

"A home-cooked meal? I'm envious."

"Then you can go in my place."

"You don't want to eat with your family?" He pulled an apple from the bag and polished it on his sleeve, apparently not planning to leave anytime soon.

"Not particularly."

"Want me to help you come up with an excuse to miss it? Some case-related emergency that I need your help with?"

"I thought you said you didn't make a habit of lying."

"I don't, but it's not lying if we actually do whatever it is I come up with." He eyed her steadily, his gaze direct and serious. He'd do it. She knew he would. And knowing it only made her wish that she could let him.

Of course, she couldn't. She had to stay in the same house with her father. It was better to just go along with the plan. "That's okay. I'll manage."

"Want me to come along?"

"Susan did say to bring a friend. So, if you really want to…" She stopped speaking as she realized what she'd done. Issued an invitation to dinner. That was a lot more like a date than she was comfortable with. "What I mean is—"

"That you need someone to run interference with your step-mother and father tonight? I can do that." The humor in his eyes was unmistakable.

"Just forget it, Cahill. Susan can set the table for nine or eleven or whatever uneven number she was trying to avoid." She flicked her ponytail over her shoulder and took a step away.

Harrison grabbed her arm lightly and pulled her to a stop. "What time?"

"What?" She looked into his eyes, saw compassion in his gaze.

"What time is dinner?"

"Harrison—"

"I've got nothing to do tonight but hang out in Vera Peel's relic of a house. Are you really going to leave me to suffer through that?"

Say yes. Tell him that he wouldn't be suffering any more than she was.

"Seven."

"How about I meet you here at six-thirty? I'll follow you over to your father's house.

"Thanks."

"Don't thank me until after I get through the meal without

offending anyone. I'd better head over to the coroner's now. See you later." He released his hold on her arm and left.

Jodie stood where she was for several minutes. Off-balance. Confused. Unsure of how she'd gone from wanting to avoid Harrison to having dinner with him.

She frowned, frustrated with herself for spending valuable time thinking about a man who meant nothing to her. A man who wouldn't ever mean anything to her.

Liar.

The accusation whispered through her mind as she went into Sam's office and grabbed the phone number for Leah Farley's brother, Clint Herald, from the desk.

FOURTEEN

Asking Leah Farley's brother, Clint, for Leah's blood type wasn't something Jodie relished doing, but she had learned early that putting off difficult things only made them harder to do. Whether she called Clint now or later wouldn't make any difference in the outcome of the case, but putting off the task wouldn't make it go away. The longer Clint waited for news, the more frustrated he'd become. In Jodie's experience, frustration could very quickly lead to anger. The last thing she wanted to do was deal with an angry man. She'd spent too much of her childhood doing that.

She dialed the number quickly, bracing herself to deal with all the questions she knew she'd be asked. Questions she still had no answers to.

"Hello?" The voice was deep and masculine, confident and with just a hint of impatience to it.

"May I speak to Clint Herald?"

"Speaking." There was a weary tone to the man's voice, and Jodie suspected that he'd been receiving calls from friends, family and news reporters constantly since his sister's disappearance.

"This is Agent Jodie Gilmore with the Federal Bureau of Investigation. I wanted to touch base with you regarding your sister's case."

"You're the lady who grew up in Loomis."

"That's right."

"So you know my sister would never run away from her problems. She'd never murder someone. And she would never, ever abandon Sarah, her daughter."

"She was a year ahead of me in school. We didn't hang out in the same circles." And Jodie had been too busy finding trouble to pay much attention to the people in school.

"Right. I shouldn't have assumed, but I'm desperate. My sister is out there somewhere, and it doesn't seem like you people are doing much to find her."

"We've launched a full investigation—"

"Which has yielded nothing."

"We know that there was an argument between your sister and her husband. We know that Sarah is afraid of women with red hair. We also found your sister's shoe. We now know the blood on it wasn't her husband's."

"There was never any doubt about that, Agent Gilmore."

"Leah's husband is dead. Murdered, Mr. Herald. Your sister is gone. Whether or not she committed the crime is something we are obligated to investigate."

He sighed, and Jodie knew he was reeling in his anger. "I know. I wouldn't expect any less, but Leah has a kid. A little girl, who desperately misses her mother. We need her home."

"I understand." Jodie took a deep breath, not wanting to continue, but knowing she had to. "Mr. Herald, do you know your sister's blood type?"

The silence on the other end of the line lasted several heartbeats. Then Clint spoke, his voice tight. "Do you think the blood on the shoe is Leah's?"

"We don't know, yet. Even if it is—"

"She's alive. I know it."

Jodie had heard so many others say the same. People who

truly believed that nothing bad could happen to someone they loved. Sometimes they were right. Most often, they weren't. "We're all hoping the same thing. Right now, we've got no reason to believe otherwise. Do you know her blood type?"

"I think it was B positive, but I'm not sure. The hospital should have the information."

Jodie's heart sank at his words, but she wouldn't tell him that the blood type found on the shoe matched his sister's. There was no sense giving him that information until they were sure the blood was Leah's. "I'll check with the hospital to find out for sure. In the meantime, do you have access to a brush that might contain Leah's hair?"

"You're going to do DNA testing." It wasn't a question, but Jodie answered anyway.

"Yes."

"I'll see if I can find one. If I do, I'll drop it off for you."

"Thank you for your help, Mr. Herald."

"Keep me updated." He hung up the phone before Jodie could respond.

It was for the best. She couldn't make promises, and there was little she could add to what had already been said. His sister was missing. If the blood on the shoe was hers, they'd begin looking for a body rather than a missing person.

She didn't like the thought and grabbed her jacket. Maybe the hospital would say Leah's blood type was A or O or something other than B positive. If Jodie called, she'd be put on hold. She'd go there instead. Maybe by the time Sam returned from New Orleans, she'd have more than vague speculations to go on.

Harrison was running late. Caught up in re-creating the face of John Doe, he'd let the afternoon and evening slip away. At ten till seven, he was just pulling up in front of headquarters.

To his surprise, Jodie's car was still there, the low-slung sporty vehicle gleaming beneath the streetlight. He'd thought she might leave without him. Had almost hoped she would. She'd seemed reluctant to accept his company, but the look in her eyes had said she needed him there. Harrison had come to Loomis to do a job, but when he was with Jodie, he wondered if God had brought him there for other reasons.

He pushed open the door and stepped into headquarters, his eyes scanning the room until he caught sight of Jodie seated at a desk on the far side of the room, papers spread out in front of her. His pulse jumped in acknowledgement, and he knew he was in more trouble than he'd imagined when Sam Pierce had called and asked him to come to Loomis.

Jodie looked up as he walked toward her, her eyes deep blue and darkly shadowed. "Is it that time already?"

"It's past that time. I'm running late."

"Are you kidding?" She glanced at the clock on the wall and scowled, gathering the papers, putting them in a file folder and placing them in a file cabinet. "Great. My father doesn't tolerate tardiness. I'll be raked over the coals for the first ten minutes of dinner."

"We could always skip."

"You can skip it. I have to sleep in Dad's house tonight." She stood and stretched, wincing a little.

"Been sitting too long?"

"Yeah. I keep going over Leah's file, thinking we missed something or someone, but there's nothing."

"Did you get her blood type?"

"I did. It's not good news for her family."

"I'm sorry."

"I called Sam and told him that we'll need to go ahead and run the DNA test. Leah's brother brought a brush with hair samples by, so hopefully we'll know for sure soon."

"How did her brother take the news?"

"He won't even consider the fact that his sister might be dead. As far as he's concerned, the blood on the shoe isn't hers."

"When it's family, we sometimes see with blinders on."

"I know. I just wish I could give Clint the answers he needs."

"That's what I say every time I start a case. If I can just give the families answers, they can go on with their lives. It's the not knowing that keeps people from moving forward."

"That's for sure. Let me run a brush through my hair and then we'll leave. If I don't, my father will give me grief for not being 'presentable.'"

"Hopefully, he won't kick me out for dressing like this." Harrison glanced down at his polo-style shirt and faded jeans. Not the best thing to show up to dinner in, but not the worst.

"You'll be fine. My father takes pride in being very charming to the people he meets."

"But not to you?"

Jodie shrugged, freeing her hair from its ponytail and pulling a brush through it, unwilling, it seemed, to discuss her relationship with her father.

He didn't ask again, just watched as she ran the brush through her thick hair. When he'd met her, he'd thought her young and inexperienced, but she didn't seem that way now. Now she seemed more mature, intelligent, alluring. The kind of woman he wouldn't mind spending more time with.

"Okay. I'm ready. Don't expect much in the way of cheerful conversation at dinner. If memory serves, the meal is usually as silent as a tomb." She shoved the brush back in her purse, her cheeks pink.

Obviously, she'd sensed his scrutiny and was embarrassed by it. "I'm not concerned about conversation. I'm more interested in whether or not the food is edible."

She laughed, but the shadows in her eyes remained. "Don't

worry about that. Susan said they have a chef, and I know my father would never pay someone to cook inedible food."

"Then let's go. From the sound of it, your father isn't going to hold dinner for us. If there's no food left, I'll be forced to eat out again." He took her elbow, feeling the delicate bones beneath her suit jacket. And feeling her tension. She might be acting relaxed, but dinner with her family wasn't something she was looking forward to.

As soon as they stepped outside, she tugged away from his hold, darkness hiding her expression. "We should take two cars. I'm sure you'll want to go straight back to Vera's when dinner is over."

"Actually, I'll probably go back to the coroner's. He gave me the key and said I'm free to use the facility when I want."

"He must think highly of you."

"It's more likely that he's anxious to get me out of his hair."

A loud crash sounded from the alley beside the building, and Harrison pivoted, adrenaline racing through him as he scanned the area. "What was that?"

"I don't know, but I'm going to find out." Jodie took a step toward the alley, but Harrison pulled her up short.

"I'll go check it out."

"I'm the one carrying the gun. I think I'd better be the one to check it out."

A low-pitched scream echoed out into the street, and another crash followed, quiet sobs filling the night. Jodie raced toward the sound, her heels clicking on the pavement, her dark jacket blending into the night.

Harrison hoped she didn't think he planned to stand by the car and wait until she returned. She might be an FBI agent and well trained to face situations like this one, but he wasn't about to let her do it alone.

He raced after her, not knowing what they were going to find in the alley but sure it wouldn't be good. There had been three murders in Loomis during the past few months. Two more murders committed decades ago. He didn't know much about the little town, but what he knew told him that he wouldn't want to live there.

He didn't particularly want to die there, either.

He moved into the alley anyway, bracing himself for whatever trouble was waiting there and praying that Jodie wouldn't have to pull her gun, that shots wouldn't be fired and that the woman he was coming to admire more every day wouldn't end up lying on the ground, blood staining the pavement beneath her.

FIFTEEN

Jodie's hand hovered over her gun as she ran into the alley, her heart racing, adrenaline pounding through her, demanding action. She worked to control it, knowing it could be both friend and enemy. Innocent people could die when the urge to go in shooting took over common sense.

Right now, Jodie's mind was shouting "shoot," but her gut was saying something different. *Wait. Listen. Give things a chance to come into focus.*

Something moved in the deep shadows, a dark blur that weaved and swayed toward her.

"Freeze! FBI!" She shouted the order but still didn't pull her weapon. Whoever was there wasn't moving quickly or confidently, and she was sure she caught a whiff of alcohol on the air.

"FBI. FBI." The mumbled words were accompanied by more movement, and Jodie squinted, trying to get a clearer view.

"Sir, do you need help?"

"Yeth, help. I need help. They're comin' to get me. Comin' to get me." The man stepped out of the shadows, weaving slightly as he approached.

"Who is coming to get you?" Jodie glanced around but could see nothing but Dumpsters and litter in the narrow alley.

"There. Right there!" The man shrieked, pointing to the trash bin closest to him, his body swaying toward it.

"It's a Dumpster, sir. That's all." Still, Jodie's fingers brushed the butt of her gun, and the metallic taste of fear filled her mouth. Was there someone hiding in the shadows?

"Please, please, don't hurt me. I won't tell. I won't. Won't. I won't." The words were slurred and directed toward the Dumpster.

"Sir, let me help you." Jodie moved forward, relaxing, sure now that the man was too drunk to know fantasy from reality.

He whirled toward her, screaming, rushing forward and knocking into her as he tried to escape. Unbalanced, Jodie fell backward. Strong hands grasped her waist, holding her up when she would have tumbled to the ground.

"Careful, Gilmore." Harrison's words were warm against her ear, his fingers tightening for a second before he released his hold.

"Where'd he go?" Jodie swiveled, caught sight of the man cowering near the wall and nearly sagged with relief. A guy as drunk as this one should be taken somewhere safe until he dried out. Otherwise, he might hurt himself or someone else.

"Sir?" She approached cautiously, not wanting to frighten him more than he already was. She'd seen military veterans act in similar ways, caught up in the memories that haunted them.

"He's not hearing anything but what is in his head." Harrison moved beside her, his long stride shortened to match hers.

The man watched their approach with wide-eyed terror, his mouth hanging open as if a scream were caught inside.

"Whatever it is, it can't be pleasant. The poor guy looks like he's going to jump out of his skin. Sir? What's your name?"

"Don't hurt me."

"We're not going to hurt you. We just want to make sure you get home okay." Harrison's soothing tone seemed to register, and the man blinked.

"Do I know you?"

"No, I'm from out of town."

"Okay. Okay. Just go away then." The man crouched down, huddling close to the ground, his head on his knees.

"Tell us where you live. We'll take you home." Jodie hesitated, then put her hand on his arm, hoping the gesture would calm him. He jerked back but didn't speak.

"If you don't tell us who you are and where you live, we're going to have to call the police and have them come get you. We can't leave you here like this." Jodie thought her words would motivate him to give the information they needed.

Instead, he nodded vigorously. "The police. Get the police. I need the police."

Jodie glanced at Harrison, saw that he was watching her, his eyes glittering in the darkness, waiting for her decision in the matter. "Can you call the sheriff's department? I think we need someone to come get this guy."

"Will do." He pulled a cell phone from his pocket and dialed quickly, relaying the information and then hanging up. "Let's see if we can get him out of this alley."

"That might not be easy. The guy has obviously lost touch with reality." Jodie crouched down next to the man, trying to see if he was hurt as well as drunk. "Are you injured, sir?"

"Just take me to the police. Tell them to lock me away. Okay?" The darkness couldn't hide his bleary eyes or the soft fullness of his face. This wasn't the first time he'd been drunk, and it probably wouldn't be the last, unless he killed himself by walking in front of a car, or worse, driving one.

"Hey, buddy." Harrison pressed in close to Jodie's side, reaching out to pat the drunk on his shoulder. "Give us something to go on here, okay? What's your name?"

"I don't want to die." The words were even more slurred, and Jodie wondered how long it would be before the man fell flat on his face.

"You're not going to. Come on. Up we go." Harrison hooked an arm around the man's waist and hauled him up.

"Where we goin'?"

"To the police." Jodie grabbed the man's arm, helping to support his weight as they moved toward the front of the alley.

"You tell them what I did. Tell them to keep me in jail. Tell them."

"What did you do?" Jodie tried to see the guy's expression, but his head was down, his feet shuffling as they walked.

"Something bad. I need to be in jail. For a long time. You tell them."

"Right, buddy. Whatever you say. Just hold a little of your own weight, will you?" Harrison growled the request, his hand shifting on the drunk's waist, his knuckles brushing against Jodie's side, the contact more real than the drunk's rambling rant or the strong smell of alcohol that swirled around them.

She shivered, relieved to see a patrol car pulling up in front of headquarters as she and Harrison half-carried the drunk out of the alley.

Sheriff Reed got out of the car, frowning as Jodie and Harrison got closer. "You at it again, Chuck?"

"You need to throw the book at me, Sheriff. Throw me in jail. Throw me in and toss the key. Don't let me out. Don't let me out ever."

"No need for such drastic measures. We'll just keep you until you sober up. By tomorrow morning you'll be out looking for your next shot of whiskey, and Vera can come pick you up and bring you back to her place. You're still working for her, right?" Sheriff Reed opened the back door of his car and gestured for Jodie and Harrison to help the man into it.

"She can't help me, you see? You need to keep me. Keep me there for a long, long time. Keep me—" The sheriff shut the door on his ranting passenger and turned to Jodie.

"Looks like you met the town drunk."

"Drunk, and troubled. Why is he so determined to go to jail?" In all the time she'd been working as an officer of the law, Jodie had never met someone who wanted to be locked up.

"Who knows? The guy drinks like a fish. It's pickled his brains."

"I've known people who have been a lot more drunk than this guy, Sheriff. I can't remember any of them wanting to go to jail. He must have a reason." Harrison said what Jodie was thinking, and she smiled in his direction, glad she didn't have to go head to head with the sheriff alone.

"Sure, he's got a reason. He wants a couple of free meals. Give him a day without booze and he'll be begging to get out." Sheriff Reed sounded more annoyed than concerned, and Jodie tensed. How many times had he treated her the same way when she was a teenager? Acting more annoyed than concerned when he'd spotted her wandering through town after a fight with her father, reading her the riot act when she'd been picked up for truancy but never checking with her father to find out why Richard hadn't cared.

"I'm not sure that's all there is to it. He's terrified." She tried to keep the anger out of her voice, but failed.

"Look, missy, just because you grew up around here doesn't mean you've got the right to tell me how to do my job."

"I'm not telling you how to do anything. I'm suggesting that as a law enforcement officer, you have an obligation to investigate the concerns of all of the citizens of Loomis. Drunk or not." Her hands were fisted so tightly they were numb, and Jodie knew that despite years spent trying to put the past behind her, she still hadn't managed to let it go.

"You're here to find Leah Farley, not stick your nose into other cases. Not that this is a case. It's just a drunk guy who's paranoid. Same kind of people are all over this country. I don't see as how that's something to get all up in arms about."

"I'm not—"

"Don't we have a dinner engagement, Jodie?" Harrison linked his fingers with hers and squeezed lightly, saying without a word that arguing with the sheriff was useless.

He was right.

Reed's only agenda was to keep his life as easy as possible until his upcoming retirement. Looking into a drunk's paranoid ramblings would take too much time and effort.

Jodie took a deep breath and forced a smile. "Right. We'd better get going. Thanks for coming out to help, Sheriff."

"No need to thank me for doing my job." The sheriff got in his car and drove away, not bothering to say goodbye.

"Are you okay?" Harrison's thumb stroked the inside of her wrist, the caress soothing.

"Fine."

"Then why do you look like you'd tear Reed's head off if you could?"

"He's lazy. That's not a good quality in a law enforcement official."

"You're right, but I think something more than that is bothering you."

"I guess you're going to tell me what." Despite her frustration, Jodie began to relax, the flow of the conversation, the ease of Harrison's company, the gentle touch on her wrist reminding her that she wouldn't always be back in Loomis. That eventually she'd get back to the life she'd built and away from the ugly, spiteful little town she'd grown up in.

"I would, but we're already late, and I'm hungry." He smiled, his thumb smoothing over her wrist one last time before he released his hold. "How about we discuss it after dinner?"

"Dinner! What time is it?" She glanced at her watch, her

heart sinking when she saw the time. "Great. We're a half an hour late."

"And? You had an emergency. I'm sure your father and step-mother will understand."

"You're sure because you've never met my father."

"I guess we're about to remedy that situation. Ready to go?"

No, but of course she would. As she'd told Harrison earlier, she didn't have a choice. Not when she was going to be spending another night in her father's house. "As ready as I'll ever be."

"Are you always this gloomy, Gilmore?"

The question took Jodie by surprise. She'd never thought of herself as gloomy. Most of the time she had a positive outlook. It was what had gotten her through the years when she'd lived on peanut butter sandwiches and macaroni dinners. It was what she'd leaned on when she'd felt most alone. Things would get better. They always did. At least that's what she told herself. Until she'd returned to Loomis. The town seemed to suck the life and energy out of everyone in it.

"Not usually. This case is just…stressful."

"Because you're home?"

"This has never been home." She opened her car door and got in. "Just follow me over. It's not far."

He nodded, his eyes probing hers, searching for answers she had no intention of giving. The past was just that. Studying it, rehashing it, worrying about it was something Jodie didn't want to do.

So why was it all she'd done since she'd come to Loomis?

She sighed and closed the door, turning on the engine and pulling away from headquarters. A few hours in her father and stepmother's presence. She'd made it through FBI training. She could make it through that. Then she would lock herself in the guest room, pull the covers over her head and try to forget all the reasons why she should never have come back here.

SIXTEEN

There were two cars parked in her dad's driveway when Jodie arrived. Two couples? They were probably people who had known Jodie during her rebellious years. That wouldn't be so bad if Harrison weren't attending the dinner. But he was, and Jodie was sure he'd spend the evening being entertained with stories of her childhood indiscretions. She, on the other hand, would spend the evening wishing it were over.

She got out of the car, waiting while Harrison parked his car, and then walking to the front door with him. She'd barely tapped on the door when it opened and Susan appeared.

"Jodie! You're here. I was worried you weren't going to make it. Come into the dining room. The chef is just serving." She paused, her gaze jumping to Harrison. "And you've brought a friend. Wonderful."

"This is Harriso—"

"We'll save the introductions for later. You know how impatient your father can be." Susan smiled an apology as she hurried them into the dining room.

The room had been built to entertain, the table large enough to seat ten people. At some point the beige carpet Jodie remembered from childhood had been replaced by hardwood, the cream walls painted a muted yellow.

"So, my daughter finally deigns to grace us with her presence. I'm glad you made it, my dear." As always, Richard kept his barbs carefully hidden in front of others.

"I apologize for our lateness. There was an emergency that needed to be dealt with." She slid into the seat that Susan indicated, scanning the people in attendance. Some looked familiar. Others didn't. It would be interesting to see if anyone brought up the Leah Farley case and even more interesting to hear what people had to say about it if someone did. One lead would make up for the torture she was about to go through.

Maybe.

"Who is your friend? Another FBI agent?" Richard smiled in Harrison's direction, the epitome of polite host, but the predatory gleam in his eyes told a different story.

No, Dad, he's a serial killer I picked up while working on another case.

Jodie had the fleeting urge to say exactly what was going through her head, but she wasn't a brash and troubled kid anymore. She'd spent ten years learning to control her tongue. She wasn't going to ruin it now by stepping into the trap she was sure her father was laying for her.

"Actually, Harrison is a forensic anthropologist who we've called in to work on the case."

"We? I thought you'd just started helping with the case. Now you're telling me that you're the one calling the shots. Fascinating." Richard laughed and shook his head.

Jodie's cheeks heated, but she refused to rise to the bait.

"Dad, maybe you could introduce Harrison to your friends."

"Of course. Harrison, these are Mark and Nancy Hill and Pat and Nora Millstream. Friends from church."

Jodie remembered the Millstreams. The full-cheeked woman and beer-bellied husband had been over often when she was a kid.

"It's nice to meet all of you." Harrison's voice was tight, but he smiled the same charming smile he'd used on Vera.

"It's good to meet you, too. We were so excited when we heard a big-city forensic scientist had come to town." Nora nearly vibrated with enthusiasm, her small dark eyes focused on Harrison. Maybe dinner wouldn't be so bad after all. If they concentrated on Harrison, there might not be any interest in commenting on Jodie's teenage antics.

"I'm glad I could be here to help out."

"The FBI apparently needs as much help as it can get. They've been investigating for months and we still have a woman missing and several unsolved murders."

"Maybe with Jodie here that will change."

"Jodie?"

"She is an FBI agent."

"Yes, well, you have to understand that we knew her when she was young. It's hard to think of her as more than a kid."

"Did you know her mother?" At Harrison's question the room went silent, every eye turning to him. He didn't even have the good grace to look embarrassed. Instead, he waited until the chef set salads in front of each guest, then continued. "I've heard that Jodie looks a lot like her mother. I was wondering if it was true."

"What does that have to do with anything?" Richard nearly growled the words, all his charm gone.

"Maybe I'm just curious. Jodie is an interesting woman. I'm assuming her mother—Amelia, wasn't that her name?—was, too."

"Interesting? Both of them were more trouble than they were worth." The venom in Richard's voice made Jodie wince, and she turned her attention to her salad, knowing there was nothing she could say to calm her father. Even if there was, she wouldn't have tried. Let her father show his true colors for a change. Let the people who admired his business sense, his charitable gifts, his charming exterior see what he was really like.

She should have known that wouldn't happen.

He took a deep breath his ruddy face relaxing. "Sorry. That didn't come out the way I meant it to. Amelia's betrayal affected me deeply. Let's ask God's blessing on the food, and then we can eat."

Jodie bowed her head, and for the first time in years considered actually praying. Sometimes, if she thought about it enough, she was sure God must be near, concerned and listening, wanting the best for her. If He was, if He did, surely He'd be willing to get her out of dinner with Richard, Susan and their friends.

She didn't pray, though. Too much time had passed since the days when she'd sent impassioned pleas to the heavens. God hadn't listened then. There was no reason to believe He'd listen now.

Was there?

The question echoed through her mind as Richard ended his blessing and dug into his salad. Within minutes he was also digging into Jodie, regaling his guests with humorous tales of the trouble she'd been in when she was a kid, reminding anyone who would listen that he hadn't seen his only daughter in ten years. He didn't mention that was the way he preferred it.

Jodie's head throbbed more with every word, the ache she'd been feeling for two days turning into a full-fledged pain that speared through her right eye and lodged at the base of her skull. Still, she didn't try to stop her father's seemingly charming banter. If she listened closely enough, asked the right questions, someone in the room might reveal something about Leah Farley and her husband that could help solve the missing person's case and get Jodie out of Loomis for good.

"Feeling okay?" Harrison leaned in close, his words soft as a baby's breath, his warm palm pressing against her chilled fingers.

"Fine."

"Your dad sure does enjoy airing your dirty laundry, doesn't he?"

"You haven't heard anything yet. He's just warming up." She pushed a piece of perfectly cooked fish to the side of her plate and nodded that she was done as the chef came to remove plates.

"I was hoping he'd mention your mother again. Doesn't seem like he will."

"Dad never talks about her. He—"

"Now, now. No whispering sweet nothings at the table." Susan giggled, beaming at Jodie and Harrison. Did she think they were an item? Did it *look* like they were an item?

Of course it did.

Harrison was as good as holding her hand.

Jodie tried to shift her hand out from under his, but he just linked fingers with hers and remained exactly as he had been. "You've got a lot of cute stories about Jodie, Mr. Gilmore. I can't imagine it was easy raising your daughter alone."

"You're right about that. I've always said a girl needs her mother. Would have told Amelia that if she'd given me a chance."

"She didn't tell you she was leaving?" Harrison took a sip of water and watched Richard Gilmore's reaction. The man's stories might have been amusing, but Harrison had heard the acid tone behind them. A father who loved his daughter would never embarrass her the way Richard was embarrassing Jodie. And there was no doubt she was embarrassed.

Her cheeks were blazing, her lips pale. From the looks of things, she was ready to leave, but he knew she wouldn't.

Harrison was sure she had the same idea he did—get information from the people there, see if it had any bearing on the cases they were investigating.

"Tell me she was leaving? She'd told me she was staying.

That she planned to rent a house in town. I should have known it was a lie. Every word that woman ever spoke was."

"Richard, you know that's not true." Nora Millstream cut in, her gaze darting to Jodie, her full cheeks pink.

"Maybe I'm exaggerating a little." Richard shrugged, shoveling desert into his mouth with gusto. He looked well fed and pampered. Not the kind of guy who'd been emotionally scarred by his wife's betrayal.

"A little? Amelia was a wonderful woman. Just wonderful. And she loved Jodie. I can remember her coming for tea with the ladies' Bible study. She'd always bring you, Jodie."

Harrison felt Jodie's muscles tense, her hand beneath his jerked, then settled down again. "Did she? I didn't know that."

"Oh, she did. Everywhere she went, you were right there with her. You even had matching outfits. Flowered dresses. Yellow ones with little purple flowers all over them. So cute."

"I don't remember much about my mother." Despite her obvious discomfort, Jodie stepped into the conversation.

"Of course not. You were so young when she left. I'll tell you, I was shocked to hear that she'd just walked away." Nora shook her head. "I just didn't think Amelia had it in her to do that. Just like Leah Farley. I never would have expected her to leave her daughter, but she did."

"You knew her well?"

"Not as well as I knew your mother. Amelia and I were friends. What a hard summer that was." Nora sighed and shook her head. "First, your mother leaving. Then Mary's death. A few days after that, Vera called hysterical because her husband had left her."

"You said my mother left before Mary died. Was it a week before? A month? A few days?

"Just the day before. I remember it very specifically because I was thinking how sad it was that two girls in two days would lose their mothers."

"You know, it's been such a long day. I don't want to be rude, but I think I'll get a breath of fresh air and then head to bed." Jodie pushed away from the table, and Harrison followed.

"I'll join you outside."

"It's okay, Cahill. Stay and chat for a while."

Did she really think he would do that? "Mr. and Mrs. Gilmore, thank you for your hospitality. Dinner was delicious."

"Call me Richard. And there's no need for you to run off just because Jodie is too tired to be polite. Stay and have some after-dinner port with us."

"Thanks, but I think I'll pass on it this time." Harrison said a quick goodbye to the rest of the guests, then strode out of the dining room. Cavernous and sterile, the house reminded him of a museum filled with beautiful, untouchable things. In some ways it reminded him of Jodie. Her quiet beauty begged attention, but she seemed reluctant to accept it. After meeting her father, Harrison could understand why. Every word the man had spoken about his daughter had been either a spite-filled joke or an out-and-out insult.

The exterior door closed quietly, and Harrison knew Jodie was already outside, walking away from the house and the pain her father seemed so determined to heap on her. A small part of him wanted to get in the car and drive away, let her have the space she wanted. The larger part, the part willing to acknowledge that his plans weren't always the best ones, that sometimes God had something different in mind, made him push open the front door and search the darkness.

The air was ripe with rain, dark clouds covering the moon and stars, the blackness of night silky and alive. Harrison inhaled deeply, enjoying the peace of the small town despite the secrets he knew it contained.

Jodie was a dark shadow against the blackness, moving down the sidewalk away from the house. If she heard him approaching, she didn't acknowledge him, and Harrison knew she'd rather he leave than follow. He moved up beside her anyway. "You were right about your dad."

"I was right about my mom, too. She really was lying in that tunnel for twenty-five years." Her voice was rough with emotion, her head down, her hair falling in a pale curtain around her face.

"You don't know that."

"I do know it, Harrison. So do you."

"What I know is that no matter what we find, you're going to be okay. You're a strong woman. Nothing that happens can take that away from you."

"Strong? Right now, all I feel is tired."

"Maybe you just need someone to lean on for a while." He put his hands on her shoulders and turned her around, looking down into her face and seeing the tears in her eyes.

"The problem with leaning on someone, Cahill, is that if you do it too long, you forget how to stand on your own."

"That will never happen to you, Jodie." He brushed her silky hair away from her face, his hand cupping the nape of her neck as he pulled her into his chest.

She stiffened, then relaxed, her head resting against him, her breath coming out in a deep shuddering sigh.

"I've spent twenty-five years despising my mother for abandoning me. If she didn't…"

"Then you'll know the truth. Everyone deserves that."

"There's a connection, you know. Between my mother's murder and Mary Sampson's." She spoke quietly but didn't move away.

"If Jane Doe is your mother."

"She is." She pulled back, but Harrison couldn't quite make himself let her go.

"There's someone else that may be connected."

"Vera's husband."

"Right. I think it's interesting that he walked out on her just a few days after two women were murdered."

"I'd like to speak with him. Maybe Vera will have his contact information." Jodie's hand had come to rest on his arm, the warmth of it seeping through his shirt, reminding him of all the things he'd thought he would have with Allison. Love, companionship, family. When they'd broken up, he'd been more relieved than brokenhearted. He had a feeling that wouldn't have been the case if the woman he'd lost was Jodie.

"I'll try to get it from her tonight. If I don't show up for work tomorrow, you'll know what happened."

"Don't even joke like that, Cahill. With all the murders that have taken place in this little town, it's not funny." Jodie's face was set in somber lines.

"You're worried about me, Gilmore? I'm touched."

"Don't be. I'm no good at sculpting, and if something happens to you, I doubt if we can find anyone else to work this case." She grinned as her hand fell away from his side, and Harrison had the urge to grab it, tug her close and find out if her lips were as soft as they looked.

"I'll keep that in mind if the woman comes after me with a baseball bat."

"You do that." Jodie smiled again, her lips curving up, tempting Harrison to do exactly what he knew he shouldn't. Lean in. Press his lips to hers.

Maybe she sensed the direction of his thoughts. Her eyes widened. "I'd better go in. Good night, Harrison."

"Good night." He watched until she was inside, then got in his car and drove to Vera's place. A hulking shadow in the darkness, one dim light visible through a front window, the house was as uninviting as its owner. If Harrison had been the kind of person who believed in ghosts and haunts, he would have turned around and run the other way the first time he'd seen it.

It probably would have been wise. Not only was Vera the least hospitable hostess he'd ever met, but also the bed was uncomfortable, the room stuffy and the shower ran more cold than hot. He unlocked the door and stepped into the stale-smelling foyer, stopping in surprise as he caught sight of Vera hovering near the door to his room.

"Mr. Cahill, I'm glad you're back. I've got an adjusted bill for you to look over." She handed him a sheet of paper, and Harrison glanced at it.

"I appreciate it."

"Well, if you'll just keep the lights off when you're not using them, we won't have to do this again." She sniffed, her back ramrod straight.

"I'll keep that in mind." He leaned against the stair banister and tried to think of an easy way to ask what he needed to. "I was at the Gilmores' house for dinner tonight."

"Then you won't have to raid my kitchen for food."

"No, but I'm hoping I can raid your memories."

"What in the world do you mean, Mr. Cahill?" Vera's eyes were so wide, Harrison was afraid they'd pop out of her head.

"Just that I have a few questions for you."

"Very well. Go ahead."

"I heard that your husband left you twenty-five years ago."

"It's not something I talk about." Her lips tightened, and Harrison wondered if she'd walk away before he could ask more.

"I understand. It must have been a painful time."

"Painful? I had a daughter to raise. Why do you think I opened this boardinghouse? I needed an income to keep food on the table for the two of us."

"I know your daughter must appreciate what you did for her. Do you think she ever tells her father how difficult it was for you?" Not the smoothest transition, but he'd gotten things headed in the right direction.

"Her father? Perceval was not a father."

"But your daughter does have contact with him." He pressed for more despite the venom in Vera's words.

"I haven't seen or heard from Perceval since the day he left me a note and walked away. Neither has my daughter. Now, if you'll excuse me, I'm going to bed." She turned on her heels and walked up the stairs.

Harrison frowned, walking into his room. It was strange that Vera hadn't heard from her husband since he'd left. It was as if he'd disappeared, too. Just like Jodie's mother. Part of a family one day. Gone the next. Never to be heard from again.

A coincidence?

Harrison didn't know, but he planned to find out.

He sat down on the bed, reached for his laptop and scowled. He'd left the laptop closed. Now it was open. Anger filled him as he surveyed the room. His suitcase was unzipped and opened, just the way he'd left it. The clothes inside were neatly folded, but Harrison's Bible was no longer centered on top of his shirts. Instead, it had fallen to the side.

He wanted to go upstairs, knock on Vera's door and demand to know why she'd been in his room. He knew what her answer would be—she'd been cleaning, changing linens—something that would give her an excuse to snoop.

For now, he'd let it go. See what happened while he was gone the next day. He glanced at the clock, frowning when he realized how early it still was. Nine o'clock. There was no television in the room. No one he wanted to call. Okay, that wasn't quite the truth. He wanted to call Jodie and ask how she was doing. Maybe ask what she thought about Vera's snooping through his things.

Instead, he grabbed his laptop and checked his e-mails, the

house settling around him, the silence oppressive and heavy. How Vera had spent decades here he didn't know, but the sooner he could close this case and get out, the happier he'd be. He lifted his Bible, opening to the Psalms, losing himself in God's word as the night unfolded.

SEVENTEEN

Rain splattered against the roof and splashed against the windows, the torrential downpour feeding Jodie's glum mood. She pulled back the curtain, staring out into gray morning light. Water puddled onto the already-saturated ground.

She sighed, letting the curtain fall back. Sunday morning. A day to sleep in. To enjoy. She wasn't doing either. At just past seven, she was wide-awake, the migraine she'd been fighting since she'd arrived in town three days ago back with a vengeance.

Anxiety did that to her, and she'd been plenty anxious since she returned to Loomis. Despite spending the previous day questioning Leah Farley's friends and relatives, she'd made no headway on the case.

A soft knock sounded at the door, and Jodie pulled it open, glad for the distraction. She smiled when she saw Susan dressed in a silky robe, her hair slightly tousled. "Good morning, I hope my pacing didn't wake you."

"I couldn't hear a thing above the sound of the rain. I'm just an early riser. I was heading down to get some coffee when I saw the light under your door. Would you like to join me for a cup?"

Jodie wanted to say no. Bonding with her stepmother over

a cup of coffee wasn't on the agenda for the day. Then again, being up at seven o'clock on a Sunday morning hadn't been on her agenda, either. "Sure."

"Wonderful. Church doesn't start until eleven, so we've got plenty of time to chat. Come on down when you're ready." From the look on Susan's face, Jodie would have thought the woman had won the lottery.

"I'll be there as soon as I shower and dress."

"I'll see you in a few minutes then." Susan hurried down the hall and Jodie closed the door again, wishing she could be happier about having coffee with her stepmother. She knew Susan was trying to be a good hostess, but her efforts only made Jodie feel more out of place.

She showered and dressed quickly, towel drying her hair and leaving it loose around her shoulders. There was no sense in putting on makeup, as she had no intention of attending church. She stepped into the kitchen, the pungent aroma of coffee a comforting welcome.

"There you are." Susan looked up from a newspaper she was reading, and stood. "Let me get you a cup of coffee."

"I can get it, Susan."

"Sit down and let me do it. For all I know you'll leave tomorrow, and I won't see you again for another ten years." The words were light and teasing, and Jodie tried to respond in kind.

"Maybe only five this time."

"I really hope it won't be that long. Your father and I would love to have you come a few times a year. New Orleans really isn't far from Loomis." She placed a cup of coffee on the table, refilled a silver creamer and a small sugar dish and set both in front of Jodie.

"Susan, you're very sweet, but you know my father doesn't want me here every month or even every year." Jodie sipped black coffee, letting the bitter heat of it chase away the sadness the knowledge brought. No matter how much she told herself she didn't care, her father's indifference still hurt.

"That's not—"

"It is true."

"You just look so much like your mother. I think when your father sees you, it reminds him of things he'd rather forget." Susan placed a bowl of muffins in the middle of the table and set a small plate down in front of Jodie.

"Maybe." She took a muffin and broke it in half, inhaling the sweet scents of blueberry and vanilla. "Does my father ever talk about my mother? Has he ever said what he thinks might have happened to her?"

"Well…"

"Don't worry, I know about the affair she was having. I was just curious about who it might have been with."

"Your father has never mentioned a name. I'm sure people in town know. I've heard hints from some of the ladies in my Bible study, but I don't want to repeat gossip."

"It's not really gossip, Susan. Not if it helps our investigation."

"How could something that happened so long ago help your investigation?"

"We're dealing with a missing person's case, but that isn't the only thing we're looking into. I'm sure you heard about the bodies that were found in the tunnel near the bayou."

"I did, but was afraid to bring it up in front of you. I don't want you to think that all I want from you is information about the cases you're working on." Susan patted her hair and offered a sheepish smile.

"You're feeding me and giving me a bed to sleep in while I'm in town. I don't mind filling you in on information that is open to the public."

"Then tell me all about it. By the time you're done, your father will be awake and we can all go to church together."

Jodie froze with her coffee cup halfway to her lips. "Susan, I really don't think I'll attend today."

"What?! You simply must. Richard has been telling everyone that his famous FBI daughter is going to be at church today."

"If that's what he wanted, he should have checked with me."

"I know, but you know how he can be when he gets something in his mind. It's very difficult to persuade him that things shouldn't go exactly the way he's got it planned out."

"I'm sorry, Susan, but I'm not concerned about my father's plans or whether or not he told half the town that I was going to be at church."

"Oh, well." Susan looked at a loss for words, her cheerful expression faltering.

"I know you mean well, but you can't fix what is broken between my dad and me."

"I understand, Jodie. I really do. And I'm not trying to settle whatever is between you and Richard. The truth is—" Susan took deep breath "—I told my friends you would be there. I know it was a silly thing to do without asking, but I was so excited to finally have you home. My mouth ran ahead of my thoughts. Don't worry about it." She smiled, but it was brittle now. She'd said she'd never had children, and Jodie couldn't fault her for trying to bond with the closest thing to one she'd probably ever have.

Guilt churned in her stomach and added to the slicing pain her head. Susan had been nothing but kind. Was Jodie really going to let the poor woman down? She wanted to. She really did.

But she couldn't.

"You said service begins at eleven?"

"Yes."

"I'll be there. I'm going to take my own car, though. I may go into headquarters afterward."

"Oh, Jodie, thank you. You don't know how much it means

to me. All these years of listening to mothers talk about their kids, and I've never had anything to add to the conversation. I know it doesn't matter. I know it's foolish, but just for today, I wanted to be able to feel a little bit of what they always have." Susan's winsome smile was gone now and the sadness in her eyes made Jodie wonder what had brought Susan into her father's life and what had made her stay.

"It's not a problem. I'm looking forward to meeting some of your friends."

"And I'm sure you'll see some of your old friends, as well." Friends?

Jodie almost laughed at the idea. She'd been an outsider for as long as she could remember. "I'm sure some of the people I went to school with are still in Loomis."

"Wonderful! I'd better go get your father moving. If I don't drag him out of bed, he won't be ready when it's time to leave for church." She took a last sip of coffee and hurried out of the kitchen.

That was Jodie's cue to go back to her room. She didn't plan to be in the kitchen when Richard came down for breakfast. He'd never been a morning person, and the last thing she wanted was to go another round with him. She finished off her coffee quickly, dumped the remainder of her muffin into the trash and hurried back up to her room to get ready. If she was going to face the people who'd judged her so harshly when she was a kid, she was going to do it looking her best.

Loomis Christian Church looked exactly like she remembered. A large brick building on Church Street. Not the most original street name, but fitting. The rain had stopped and gloomy sunlight reflected off the windows, giving the place an ethereal look that Jodie knew was as much a falsehood as any.

She pulled into the parking lot, smoothing a hand over her dove-gray linen skirt, her mouth dry with anxiety. She'd dressed for success, brushed her hair until it gleamed, applied a hint of blush to her pale cheeks, tinged her lips with color and knew that none of it would be enough.

She sighed.

She did not want to do this.

Someone tapped on her window, and she jumped, her heart slamming against her ribs as she turned to face the person peering in at her. Dark hair. Black eyelashes surrounding deep green eyes. A smile that tugged at her heart, softened her defenses. Harrison.

She unrolled her window. "What are you doing here?"

"I'd say I was doing the same thing you are, but I'm heading into church service and you're still sitting in your car, so maybe I'm not. You planning on coming in?"

"I was just trying to decide if I'm up to it."

"What is there to be up to?"

"Facing the harsh judgment of Loomis, Louisiana."

"Buck up, Gilmore. You were a police officer. Now you're an FBI agent. These people have got to be easier to face than the criminals you've chased down." He leaned in, unlocked the car door and pulled it open, his words casual and teasing but his eyes filled with understanding.

She didn't want to acknowledge it or her own insecurities, so she turned away, grabbing her purse and taking a deep breath, determined to do exactly what he'd suggested—buck up. She had a case to solve. That's what she should be thinking about. That's all she should be thinking about. "One of them might *be* a criminal. Maybe even more than one of them."

"All the more reason to get ourselves in there."

"What? You think the killer is going to be racked by guilt and confess all during the altar call?"

"That would be nice, wouldn't it? But since I don't think it's going to happen, what I'm really hoping for is some juicy gossip. I get a lot of good information that way." He cupped her elbow and headed to the church, pulling her along beside him.

"You'll get plenty of it here."

"I get the impression you aren't too fond of this church."

"It's not that. It's just…" She shrugged. She'd been disillusioned, disappointed, wanting something, needing something the church had never been able to give her—acceptance.

"What?" Harrison paused with his hand on the church door, his eyes filled with color and life and the kind of hope and faith Jodie had never experienced.

"I wanted more than what I found here."

"What did you want?" He brushed hair from her cheek, his fingers lingering, warm, compelling, urging her to believe that he was on her side, backing her up, offering her what she'd never had before.

"A reason to believe I belong." The words escaped, and Jodie swallowed back more.

"Belong? Faith isn't an exclusive club, Jodie. God isn't exclusive, either."

"Maybe He isn't, but the people of Loomis are."

"There's your problem. You're worrying about people and what they think of you, but all that really matters is God. What He wants from you. What He thinks of you." He smiled, his expression so tender, so understanding that Jodie's breath caught in her throat.

His fingers dropped away and Jodie could breathe again. Think again. And what she was thinking was that she was in trouble. Not the kind of trouble she'd been in when she was kid. No, this was a completely different kind of trouble. The broken heart, never-gonna-love-again kind of trouble. The kind she should be just as afraid of getting into, but for some reason, with Harrison she wasn't.

She frowned, taking a step away from Harrison and the promises in his eyes. "We'd better get inside or we'll be late."

With that she pushed the door open and fled to the sanctuary. She slipped into a back pew as the organ began the prelude. Seconds later, Harrison slid in next to her.

"Next time, warn a guy before you take off running." He whispered in her ear, and she blushed, knowing that running was exactly what she'd been doing.

"Shhh. The service is starting."

He chuckled, the sound vibrating along Jodie's nerves and warming her. As the service began, she tried to forget that Harrison was beside her, tried not to notice the warmth of his arm pressed next to hers. It was impossible. Harrison wasn't a man who could be ignored or forgotten. He was a man who would stick in the mind and in the heart long after he walked away.

And he would walk away.

Eventually, everyone did.

The thought was sobering, and Jodie turned her attention to the reverend taking his place at the pulpit. Early forties. Tall and broad, he spoke of forgiveness, of grace, of letting go and of moving on. The words settled deep into Jodie's soul and refused to be dislodged.

She'd moved on and she thought she'd let go, but coming back to Loomis had proven otherwise. Everything she thought she'd put behind her was still there, buried deep where she didn't have to look at it, but not forgotten. And definitely not forgiven.

The altar call began, and Jodie stood with the congregation, the urge to pray stronger than it had been in years. She wasn't sure what to say or how to say it, but she knew she had to try.

Lord, I know I need to forgive the people in this town who hurt me. I know I need to forgive my parents. Please help me do that, so I can move on with my life. Help me let go of my bitterness and move forward. Help me to know You are there.

The call to worship ended, and Jodie followed Harrison into the aisle, feeling more at peace than she had in years.

EIGHTEEN

That peace lasted as long as it took her to walk outside.

"Jodie! There you are. I've been looking everywhere for you. I thought you must have decided not to come." Susan's voice carried above the din of people exiting the church, and Jodie turned to face her stepmother.

"I got here a little late."

"So did your father and I. Now he's gone off to play golf with some friends, and you've missed each other."

"It's okay. I'm sure we'll see each other later today."

"I hope so. It is been such a long time since you've been home, and I really hoped…" Her voice trailed off and she smiled. "But it's not about what I'd hoped. Did you enjoy Reverend Harmon's sermon.

"It was wonderful."

Much better than what she'd heard when she was growing up.

"Come meet my Bible-study ladies. We're all going out to lunch, and we'd love for you to join us. Unless you have plans with Harrison." Susan shot a look in Harrison's direction.

"Harrison and I aren't together." Jodie spoke quickly, realizing only too late that she'd left herself with no excuse to skip lunch.

"Oh, well, then you can have lunch with us. We're going to Vincetta's."

"That sounds—" what could she say? That she'd rather sit alone in her room than face a handful of Loomis's women? "—great."

"Wonderful. We'll meet you there at half-past noon. I've already got a table reserved. This is going to be so much fun." Susan pulled Jodie into a hug that smelled of lilac and mint, then hurried away.

"Fun. Right." Jodie mumbled the words, and Harrison laughed.

"Come on, Gilmore. It won't be that bad."

"Have you ever hung out with a bunch of Loomis ladies? There'll be more gossip exchanged than dollars on the stock market."

"There you go, getting all Southern on me again."

"What I'm getting is anxious to find Leah Farley and get out of Loomis and back to my life."

"I was thinking the same last night. Vera Peel doesn't exactly offer four-star accommodations, and I'm pretty sure she went through my things while I was out yesterday."

"Really? Why would she do that?"

"Nosiness?"

"Maybe so. My stepmother is a lot more welcoming and a lot less intrusive, but it's hard to be around my father." She tried to smile, but failed miserably.

"I know. I saw him in action, remember?"

"It's funny, when I was really little, I thought it was me. That if I were just good enough, smart enough, he'd love me the way other fathers seemed to love their kids. Eventually, I realized that nothing I could do would ever be good enough." She shrugged, knowing she needed to let it go. Wanting to let it go, and now sure she finally knew how.

"There are plenty of other people who think you're more than good enough." He pulled her car door open, waited until she got in, then leaned down to look her in the eyes. "Me for one."

"Cahill—"

"I've got to drive to New Orleans today. They've found the remains of a child and need me to do some preliminary work on it."

"You're leaving?" She should have been thrilled. With Harrison gone, she'd have one less thing to distract her, confuse her.

Interest her.

"Just for the day. I know I've got an obligation here, too, but if this is the kid the police think it is, he's been missing for six years. It's past time for his parents to have closure."

"You're a good man, Cahill." The words slipped out, the truth of them as real as the gray sky and heavy, bayou-tinged air.

"Thanks, but it's not about being good, is it? It's about being who God wants me to be." His fingers traced the line of her jaw, then dropped away. "I'll see you when I get back. Stay out of trouble."

He stepped away, waving as Jodie pulled out of the parking lot, his words echoing through her head as she drove to Vincetta's.

It isn't about being good. It's about being who God wants me to be.

Who does God want *me* to be?

As if there were some preordained purpose and plan for each person's life.

Maybe there was.

Maybe all the struggles Jodie had gone through, all the hard work and frustration, the clawing and scraping to pay the bills so she could go to school, maybe they'd all happened for a reason and a purpose. A perfect, God-ordained plan.

And coming back to Loomis? Was that part of the plan, too? Had God orchestrated things so that Jodie would return to her roots, find her mother and make peace with her father— and her past?

It was worth thinking about, but not now. She had a luncheon to attend and some Loomis ladies' brains to pick.

She pulled into an empty parking space, brushed her hair and smoothed gloss over her lips. Then she took a deep breath and got out of the car.

Susan and several other women were already seated at a large table in the middle of the restaurant, and Jodie took the seat closest to her stepmother, glancing around the table and smiling at Nora, who waved a greeting.

"Did I miss anything?"

"We were just talking about all the excitement that's been going on in town and wondering if it's going to have an impact on the Mother of the Year Pageant." Nora leaned forward, eager, it seemed, to include Jodie in the conversation.

"You think the murders will keep people from entering?"

"Not the murders alone, but I heard Jillian Morrison received a threatening note. Poor lady. Like she hasn't been through enough." Susan sighed and took a sip of water. "But let's not dwell on sad things. Not when I'm so excited that you could come to lunch. Ladies, this is my stepdaughter, Jodie."

Susan beamed from ear to ear as she made introductions, and Jodie did her best to get into the rhythm of the lunch, smiling as she greeted each of the ladies in turn. Aside from Nora, none were people she remembered.

"Look, here comes Vera!" Susan waved the gaunt older woman over, gesturing to the seat beside Jodie. "Why don't you sit next to Jodie, dear? I'm sure you remember each other from years ago."

Vera's cold gaze rested on Jodie for a moment before she nodded. "Who could forget her? She wasn't the most quiet and well-mannered child in town."

"I've grown up a lot since then, Mrs. Peel."

"Humph. Whether you have or not isn't my concern."

"That's not a very loving way to welcome someone." Nora spoke up while the rest of the group sat wide-eyed and silent, probably memorizing every word so that they could relay it later.

"I'm not trying to be rude. Just honest. Jodie was a little hooligan. She knows it. Not that I'm judging. That is how I ended up marrying Perceval." Her tone softened, her lips twisting in what might have been a smile or a grimace.

"You were a wild teenager?" Jodie didn't believe it. There was no way the buttoned-up, straitlaced woman beside her had ever had a wild side.

"Wild? Of course not. But I did like to go to the church socials. The music and laughter. All of us girls in our fancy dresses, flirting with the boys across the room." She sighed, her expression more relaxed than Jodie ever remembered seeing it.

"You met your husband at a church social?"

"She sure did. He walked in and nearly swept her off her feet." Nora relayed the information with enthusiasm. "One dance and they were in love. A month later they were married." Nora looked up at Vera then and had the good grace to stop before she told the rest of the story. The part that ended with Perceval abandoning his wife for another woman—two days after two women in town were brutally murdered.

"How long were you married, Mrs. Peel?" Jodie asked the question, doubting she'd get an answer, and nearly fell back as Vera turned on her, her eyes blazing.

"Young lady, I am still married. I do not believe in divorce."

"You mean, you and your husband never divorced?"

"We did not." She sniffed, turning away to give the waiter her order.

Jodie knew she should let the subject drop, but she couldn't. There was too much she still needed to know. Like why a woman would remain married to a man she hadn't seen in twenty-five years.

She waited until everyone had ordered and conversation began again, then turned to Vera. "Did your husband ever file papers or ask for a divorce? He did leave you, after all."

Vera stiffened, but answered. "In his note he said he was not the marrying kind. That a settled life would never suit him. I'm assuming he's lived life doing exactly what he pleases since then. Married or not."

"How long has it been since you've seen him?"

"Too long to talk about." She looked down her nose at Jodie. "And, really, it's none of your business."

"Maybe not, but it is curious, Mrs. Peel. Your husband left right around the same time as two Loomis women died."

"Are you implying—"

"Jodie—" Susan placed a hand on Jodie's arm. "This probably isn't the best time to discuss the past."

Red-faced, Jodie turned to her stepmother. "You're right. I'm sorry. I certainly didn't mean to ruin anyone's lunch."

"It's not that." Susan leaned close, speaking softly so only Jodie could hear. "I love my friends, but they do love to talk. I wouldn't want them to spread any information that you'd rather other people not hear."

Jodie almost smiled at that. The sheriff's department was giving out information as quickly as the FBI discovered it. Nothing was going to be kept under wraps for long. Still, she didn't want to ruin Susan's lunch, so she smiled and nodded. "Thanks for the reminder."

By the time lunch was over and Jodie stepped outside, rain was falling again, splattering in puddles on the ground and pooling near the curb.

Compared to New Orleans and Baltimore, Loomis was quiet, Sunday afternoon traffic trickling down the road one slow-moving vehicle at a time. At times, Jodie had longed for the slow pace of life in small-town America. She'd never longed for Loomis, though. Spite hung over the town like a dark cloud, drifting willy-nilly from house to house, destroying everything it touched.

People said it had all started years ago, when Roland Renault III had married Scooter Pershing's daughter. When Roland cheated on his wife, publicly humiliating her, the woman had committed suicide while she was pregnant. Scooter had never forgiven Roland. Nor had he ever let his children or grandchildren forget that Renaults were lying, cheating murderers. Through the years, the Pershing descendants had struck back at the Renaults any way they could—ruining business deals and reputations. Renaults and Pershings were taught from infancy to detest each other, and the feud was still being carried out by the two families' matriarchs—Charla Ranault and Lenore Pershing—today.

Being a Pershing on her mother's side, Jodie wasn't so sure that was the exact way the whole story had played out, but there were enough people who believed it that it had become truth. Truth or exaggeration, the story had certainly caused its share of trouble in Loomis, pitting family against family, friend against friend.

Maybe that had been the point of Reverend Harmon's sermon—to get his congregation to see how destructive the Pershing–Renault feud was. Jodie gave the man points for trying but doubted he'd ever really affect a change in the hearts of Loomis's people.

It *had* affected her, though, showing her clearly that she hadn't moved on, that the past still controlled her.

She needed to forgive and let go. Her prayer this morning was a start. To do that fully, she needed answers.

She could only hope she'd get them soon.

She opened her car door and got in, ready to head back to her father's house and try to catch up on sleep, but two police cars raced past, sirens screaming, lights flashing. An ambulance followed closely behind. Not her business, she knew, but with all the trouble brewing in Loomis Jodie put on her hazards and followed anyway.

NINETEEN

The emergency vehicles pulled up in front of an old Victorian house. Bicycles littered the yard and the grass had seen better days, but the hanging baskets on the porch overflowed with vibrant flowers and the porch railing was a clean, bright white. A woman sat on the lowest porch step, two children by her side. One child held a hose and was running it over the woman's head. The other ran down the steps to urge the paramedics and police to hurry.

Had the woman been burned?

Jodie got out of her car and moved toward the group, wincing as she heard the woman's high-pitched screams. Someone else was also screaming. A child. One of the officers responded to the sound, walking inside the house. Seconds later, the screaming stopped.

"What's going on?" Jodie approached a female officer who was crouching next to the woman, she flashed her badge as she asked the question.

"She was attacked as she got out of her car. Splashed in the face with something caustic. Can you turn off the water, bud?" The officer spoke to the teen who was holding the hose. Tall and gangly with red hair and freckles, the kid was as white as a ghost.

"Is she going to be okay?"

"We're going to take good care of her." The paramedics moved in, wrapping the woman in a blanket and taking her vitals.

"Were you with your mother when this happened?" Jodie spoke quietly, hoping her calm demeanor would help ease the teen's anxiety.

"No, I was inside, watching the kids. Mom ran out for some ice cream because Benjamin got an A on his spelling test."

"Kids?" Jodie glanced at the other child, a slightly younger version of his brother. "How many children are in the house?"

"Three more. I'm the oldest." The teen looked at his mother and frowned, his chin trembling with tears Jodie knew he wouldn't let fall.

"What's your name?"

"Samuel."

"Is your dad around?"

"He died two years ago."

"I'm sorry to hear that."

"It was hard, but we were all doing better. But if Mom..." His voice trailed off, and Jodie patted his arm.

"She's going to be fine. Look, she's already improving." It was true. The woman had calmed down enough to talk, and the police officer was writing in a small notebook.

"I hope so. I'm only fifteen. I can't do all this without my mom." He gestured around the yard, and Jodie had the urge to put an arm around his shoulder and tell him everything was going to be all right.

"You won't have to. You said your mom went out for ice cream. Had she just left the house when this happened?"

"No. She was coming home. She'd been gone for maybe a half hour. I was putting the baby in for a nap when I heard the car pull into the driveway. The next thing I knew, Mom was screaming. I ran out and saw something dripping off her glasses and her face, so I grabbed the hose and sprayed her. I hope I didn't make things worse."

"You probably kept her from being hurt worse." Jodie glanced at the boy's mother and saw that her face was blotchy and red, her eyes watering. "Did you see anything when you came out of the house? A car? A person?"

"Nothing. Are you sure she's going to be okay?" He stepped toward his mother. "Mom, are you okay?"

"I'll be fine, Sammy. You go inside and make sure the little ones are okay. Please?" The woman reached up to squeeze her son's hand, and Jodie's throat closed tight with emotion. *This* was what love should be.

"Are they taking you to the hospital? Maybe I should stay out here, Mom, just to make sure you're okay. I mean, if they take you away and I don't even know it—"

"If they take me, they'll let you know first. Now, take Elijah and go inside. Give everyone some ice cream."

"All right." Samuel and his brother disappeared inside the house, and Jodie crouched in front of the woman.

"How are you feeling, ma'am?"

"My face is on fire, but I think I'm going to be okay." She took a deep breath. "I just don't know what happened. One minute I'm getting out of my car, the next some maniac in a mask is throwing a bucket of bleach in my face. Thank the good Lord I decided to wear my glasses instead of my contacts and that my son is a quick thinker."

"He seems like a good kid."

"He is. So many people I know have trouble with their teens, but Samuel hasn't given me much to complain about. Last year he even nominated me for Mother of the Year."

"He didn't just nominate her. He wrote a fantastic essay on why she should win." One of the paramedics, an older man with salt-and-pepper hair, spoke as he used a saline wash on the woman's cheeks. "Brought tears to the eyes of everyone who read it."

"It was a great essay." Distracted from her pain, the woman seemed to relax. "And, you know, he was so upset that I only got runner-up that he nominated me again this year."

"You've got a great kid there, Nancy. That's for sure." The paramedic called in to the hospital, then looked into the woman's eyes. "Listen, I know you're not going to like this, but we're going to have to take you to the hospital."

"I can't go. My kids—"

"You were just saying what a great kid Sammy is. He can handle things for a while."

"I—"

"Mrs. Bailey, if it makes you more comfortable, we'll have an officer wait here until another family member can come, or until you're able to return home."

"My mother lives in New Orleans. If someone could call her…"

"We'll take care of it." The officer stepped out of the way as a stretcher was wheeled over.

"Thank you. You don't know how much better it makes me feel to know my kids are going to be okay. Can you bring Sammy out so I can tell him?" Nancy lay back on the stretcher and closed her eyes, her face blotchy, red and swelling.

As soon as her son came out to say goodbye, the paramedics wheeled the stretcher into the ambulance. As it pulled away, Jodie followed the officer across the yard. "Did she recognize the person who threw the bleach?"

"No, and she couldn't give much of a description. Medium height. Medium build. Medium weight." The officer shook her head. "Whoever it was meant to do some damage. Mrs. Bailey really is fortunate that her son thought quickly."

"Did she have any idea of who might want to harm her?"

"Not really. She said there was a strange note on her car last week. It said something like, 'Drop out of the contest before it's too late.' She thought it was a joke and threw it away."

"It was no joke. I wish she'd kept it."

"Me, too." The officer eyed Jodie curiously. "The FBI usually doesn't take much interest in these kinds of cases."

"You're right, but there are a lot of things in Loomis we are involved in right now. I wanted to see if this was going to be connected to any of them."

"So, what do you think? Is it?"

"I'm not sure. Another Mother of the Year contestant received a threatening note. It mentioned Dylan Renault and Leah Farley."

"Mrs. Bailey doesn't seem to remember anything like that."

"That doesn't mean the perpetrator isn't the same, and it doesn't mean what happened isn't somehow connected to Leah Farley's disappearance. For now, though, I'll leave the investigation to your office. Just call me if you turn up anything that seems to link the cases." She handed the officer her card, then walked back to her car.

Two Mother of the Year nominees threatened within a week of each other. It didn't seem like a coincidence, but she was confident Sheriff Reed would choose to see it that way.

Jodie grabbed her cell phone and dialed Sam's number, wanting to fill him in on what had happened.

"Pierce here."

"Sam, it's Jodie."

"Everything okay?"

"I just left the scene of a crime. A woman who is in the running for Mother of the Year had a bucket of bleach thrown in her face."

"She okay?"

"She seems to be. What is interesting is that she received a threatening note a week ago. It said that if she didn't drop out of the contest, she'd be sorry."

"Do you have the note? We can send it to our forensics team."

"The victim thought it was a joke and threw it away."

"So we've got nothing."

"Exactly. I thought you should know anyway. There's got to be some kind of connection between this crime and the other note. Whether either has something to do with the Leah Farley case remains to be seen."

"I agree. How about we take a look at things tomorrow morning, see if maybe together we can come up with some answers?"

"I'll see you then." She disconnected and tossed the phone onto the console, wishing they had more to go on. If there was a connection between the recent rash of threats in Loomis, Leah's disappearance and the recent murders, Jodie hadn't been able to find it. She'd keep looking until she did. There was no other choice.

She rubbed the back of her neck as she drove toward her father's house. It was only three. There was still plenty of time left in the day. Maybe too much time. She felt tired and out of sorts, but she didn't feel like hiding out in her room. Instead, she drove through town and to the bayou, telling herself she had no destination in mind.

It wasn't the truth.

She knew where she was going and acknowledged it as she turned into the driveway. Thunder cracked as she drove through the wooded area where the tunnel was that had hidden two bodies for twenty-five years. Lightning flashed across the sky, the beauty of it breathtaking. Jodie parked near the house, watching as the storm played out over the bayou.

Alone. Like she'd been for so many years.

Sure, she had friends in New Orleans and in Baltimore, places to go at Christmas and on vacations. It wasn't like there weren't people who cared. It was more that Jodie had never felt like she belonged. Not to her family, not to her church, not even to God.

She'd been wrong. She knew that now. She could feel it in every beat of her heart, every rumble of thunder. The truth of God's creative power and of His love. All she had to do was accept it.

"I want to, Lord. I really do. It's just so hard."

Something moved in her peripheral vision, and she turned, her heart jumping with surprise as she caught sight of a dark figure hurrying into the thick woods surrounding her.

Jodie pushed open the car door and stepped into the rain. "Hello?"

Whoever it was either didn't hear or didn't want to stop. Jodie hurried into the thick tree line. "Hello? Anyone here?"

She was sure someone was. She could feel his eyes following her movements as she stepped deeper into the trees. She searched the area for fifteen minutes but found no one. Finally, she gave up, retreating to her car and surveying the yard once again.

Everything looked like it was in order, crime-scene tape still wound around the porch posts and across the front door. Jodie did a circuit of the house, searching for signs that someone had been inside. The rain and wind were a haunting melody that played in Jodie's head as she turned to her car and dialed Sam's number again.

More than likely, a vagrant had been using the old house as a shelter from the storm, but there was another possibility, and she couldn't ignore it. Criminals often returned to the scene of their crimes in the months and even the years that followed. She might have seen a vagrant walking into the woods.

Or she might have seen a murderer.

TWENTY

It took an hour to search the house and the surrounding property. Jodie and Sam found no sign that someone had been there. No ratty blankets or piles of belongings. Nothing that would indicate a vagrant's presence.

Soaked and shivering, Jodie led Sam into the woods. "He came this way and disappeared."

"He? Are you sure it was a man?" Sam wore a rain slicker over a dark suit, a hood pulled up over his head. Smart man. If Jodie had known she'd be wandering around outside, she would have done the same. As it was, her sweater set was plastered to her body, her linen skirt sagging, her pumps ruined. Thank goodness she hadn't worn higher heels.

"All I'm sure of is that someone was here. I wish I'd done a more thorough search of the area. I'd like to have had a chat with whomever it was."

"You were smart to call me in first." He squatted down and cocked his head to the side. "Looks like there's a path through here. It's overgrown, but visible. How about we follow it and see where it goes."

He let Jodie take the lead and she walked slowly, searching the path for footprints. There were none. Not a surprise. The ground was thick with dead leaves, raindrops lying on top of the green-brown carpet. A quarter mile in, the path wound toward the bayou, the scent of swamp heavy in the air.

Jodie wrinkled her nose, pushing through brambles and stepping out onto a gravel road that ended abruptly at the swamp.

"An access road for fishermen and their boats." She spoke mostly to herself as she scanned the area, looking for tread marks. "Anyone could have driven a car down this way, parked it and walked to the house. On a day like this, there isn't much likelihood he'd be seen."

"Lots of people are curious about the case."

"And one person is probably wondering what kind of evidence we found." Jodie frowned. "I wish I'd gotten a better look."

"If wishes were horses…"

"Beggars would ride. Right." Jodie wiped rain from her face, looked around one more time. "I guess we'd better head back."

"Yeah, my fiancée is probably wondering why I'm not back yet."

"You were on a date?" Jodie moved back into the woods, her low-heeled shoes sinking more into the ground with every step.

"We were having lunch at her place, discussing what's going to happen when the FBI calls me back to New Orleans."

"Is she going to stay here?" Jodie hoped not. Sam seemed to really love his fiancée. She'd hate for Loomis to ruin that.

"Probably not. She thinks she can move closer to New Orleans and still have her practice here."

"That would be good for both of you."

"It would. And I think it's going to happen sooner rather than later. The case here is getting cold. Aside from the shoe, we haven't found anything that might lead us to Leah. Even if the blood on the shoe is hers, and there's no solid proof of that yet, we've got no evidence to lead us to any conclusions about what might have happened to her."

"We do have the threats against Mother of the Year contestants. Although, my gut feeling on that is that it's not related to Leah's disappearance."

"Yeah, I'm feeling the same way. Someone is probably using the Loomis crime wave to scare her competitors."

"Not just scare them. Nancy could have been seriously hurt."

"True, but that's not our jurisdiction. It's up to Sheriff Reed to figure out the who and why of what's going on there. Same goes for what we found here. We found the bodies, we called Harrison in to help, but Sheriff Reed has made it pretty clear to me that the case isn't ours and he doesn't want our help on it."

"Because he doesn't want to be bothered."

"That may be true, Jodie, but it's not a federal crime, and we've got no choice but to leave it alone." They'd reached the cars, and Sam waited while Jodie got into hers. "I know this is hard for you, but in this case, you're an agent first. Then a daughter."

A daughter. The words were a blow to the chest, and Jodie winced away from them.

"Understood. I'll see you tomorrow." She closed the door and drove away, her clothes sticking to her skin, chilling her.

She barely noticed.

Agent first. Daughter second. Sam didn't understand just how easy that was. In her memory, she'd never been anyone's daughter. To her father, she'd been an inconvenience. To his wives, she'd been a troubled child they steered clear of.

And what had she been to the woman who'd given birth to her?

Nora had mentioned matching dresses and days spent together. Jodie would give a lot for one memory of those things. All she had were vague images. A woman with blond hair. A bracelet in a picture. A soft song drifting through the darkness.

She shook her head, trying to dispel the memories and the sadness that went with them. Sam had said Leah Farley's case was cold, that he thought they'd be going back to New Orleans soon. She was glad, but a small part of her didn't want to leave. Not until she knew for sure that Jane Doe was her mother, and not until she'd found the person who had killed her.

She sighed, pulling into her father's driveway and staring at the house. She'd grown up here but felt no connection to it. Nor was she connected to her father. She'd admit it. When she'd found out she was going to be working in Loomis, there'd been a small part of her that had hoped for reconciliation. A larger part, the part that knew her father would never change, understood that wouldn't happen.

She wasn't disappointed. Just resigned.

Chilled to the bone and exhausted, she stepped into the large foyer, listening to the silence of the house. Obviously, Susan wasn't home yet. If she were, Jodie knew she'd run to say hello. Like she cared. Maybe even like family.

Richard, on the other hand, could be in his den just off the foyer and wouldn't bother acknowledge her.

She kicked off her shoes and stood, dripping water onto the floor for several minutes. When she was dry enough not to leave a trail of water, she hurried up the stairs and changed, grabbing a towel from the linen closet and returning to the foyer to wipe up the puddle she'd left near the door.

The laundry room was off the kitchen and she went there, throwing the towel into the washing machine and tossing her skirt into the trash can. It was beyond repair, spotted with mud, torn by thorns.

She'd liked that skirt, too.

A crumpled piece of paper lay near the garbage can, apparently tossed and forgotten. Jodie picked it up, the bright pink paper crushed into a tight ball. Curious, Jodie smoothed it out saw the advertisement for the Mother of the Year Pageant. It was doubtful Richard had thrown it away, but she could imagine Susan going through her husband's pockets, finding a folded paper, reading it and throwing it away—trying to forget what she'd never be.

An image flashed through Jodie's mind of Susan at lunch introducing her. My stepdaughter, she'd said. Not Richard's daughter. Not my husband's daughter.

My stepdaughter. Her eyes glowing, her face beaming with happiness, as if she'd finally been included in that exclusive Loomis club—motherhood. And suddenly Jodie knew that no matter when she returned to New Orleans, no matter how much she longed to put Loomis behind her, she'd keep in touch with Susan. She'd come back for Christmas. Maybe for Easter. She'd send a card on Mother's Day and on Susan's birthday. Call more often. Put up with her father's sly barbs and overt insults. Because Susan hadn't just wanted to be part of the club, she wanted what Jodie had wanted—to belong, to be accepted, to have someone she connected with.

If God had brought Jodie to Loomis for a purpose, that must be part of it. To give Susan what she'd probably spent years praying for. To give Jodie something to come home to. To create good memories in a place filled with bad ones.

Closure. Peace.

If that was all Jodie got, it should be more than enough.

Dinner was served promptly at seven. Not a fancy fish dinner like the previous night, but a cold chicken salad served with fresh baked French bread.

"This is delicious, my dear." Richard's compliment took Jodie by surprise, and she looked at her father, seeing for the first time the age that showed clearly on his face. Lines. Sags. A softness that hadn't been there before.

"Thank you, Richard, but it was no effort at all to make. Chef left roasted chicken in the fridge. I just stirred in a few extras to add some fanciness." Susan's cheeks were pink, her eyes glowing with happiness. Obviously, there was love in this relationship. Another surprise. Most of Richard's relationships started falling apart after the first year.

"But the bread is all your doing, Susie. And you know how I love fresh baked bread."

"It is delicious, Susan."

The phone rang, interrupting the conversation, and Susan hurried to answer it. "Hello? Yes, of course. I'll get her for you." She put her hand over the mouthpiece. "Jodie, it's Harrison."

"Thank you." She stood, taking the phone, but stiffening as her father barked from the table.

"It's dinnertime, Jodie. I think your phone call can wait."

"Richard, she's here on business. She can't just not take the call. It might be important."

Richard grumbled but didn't say anything else as Jodie retreated to the kitchen and lifted the receiver to her ear. She felt like a teenager with her first crush, her breath coming a little too fast, her pulse racing. "Hello?"

"Jodie? It's Harrison."

"Is everything okay?"

"I finished things up more quickly than I thought. I'm on my way back to Loomis. Can I stop by for a few minutes?" His voice was tight, and Jodie knew without asking that he'd gotten the DNA results.

Did they match?

She wanted to ask, but the words stuck in her throat, throbbing in time with her racing pulse. "Sure. How far away are you?"

"Twenty minutes. I should be at your dad's place by seven-thirty."

"If you'd rather, I can meet you at headquarters."

"No. Stay there. I'll be there soon." He hung up, and Jodie went back to the dining room, numb. Scared.

She'd known what the results would be. She had known

from the moment she'd seen the long strands of blond hair that her mother had never left Loomis.

The thought sickened her.

"Is everything okay, Jodie? You look pale." Susan's concerned gaze rested on her as she slipped back into her seat.

"I'm fine. Harrison is on his way back from New Orleans. He's going to stop by for a while."

"I'm watching the news after dinner. I hope you don't expect me to entertain him." Richard's grumpy response seemed more habit than anything, and Jodie didn't even bother acknowledging it.

She stood and lifted her plate. "I think I'll wait for him on the porch. Thanks for the delicious meal, Susan."

"But you've barely eaten, and I've got apple cobbler in the oven and some wonderful vanilla ice cream to go with it." Susan's face fell, and Jodie wished she could sit at the table and pretend everything was okay. But she didn't think she was that good of an actress, and she couldn't dodge questions for the next twenty minutes.

"Let her be, Susan. Jodie doesn't much like to be around other people." Richard's words made Jodie's cheeks flame, but she smiled at her stepmother.

"I had such a big lunch this afternoon that I'm not hungry. You've been feeding me so well since I arrived. Usually, I just do canned soup or a sandwich. I'll have some cobbler when I come back in."

"That's a wonderful idea. Harrison can join you. I'll just leave it on the stove." Susan looked so happy at the thought Jodie didn't have the heart to tell her that Harrison was coming on official business.

She rinsed her plate and put it in the dishwasher, then stepped out onto the porch, letting night air cool her cheeks. Rain fell more softly than it had when she'd been leading Sam through the woods, pattering on the ground. Gentle. Quiet. Peaceful. Teardrops falling from heaven, as if God were crying for her, as if His pain over her loss was as deep as her own.

A silly thought, she knew, but she let it fill her as she waited, watching the street for the first sign of Harrison's headlights.

TWENTY-ONE

Jodie was standing on the porch of her father's house as Harrison pulled into the driveway, and he tensed, knowing what he had to say would break her heart. The DNA tests on Jodie and her mother were in. They were a match.

Jane Doe was Amelia Pershing Gilmore.

Gone for twenty-five years, but not really gone from Loomis at all.

Murdered. Her body lying abandoned.

It wasn't news he wanted to give, but it wasn't news he could postpone, either. Like the family of the child whose remains he had identified through dental records earlier that day, Jodie deserved to hear the news immediately. Only then could she have closure.

She watched him as he got out of his car, her face a pale oval in the dim outside light, her hair loose around her shoulders, a silken blanket he wanted to bury his hands in. "Have you been out here long?"

"Just a few minutes. You made it here quickly. I hope you didn't speed to do it."

"There wasn't much traffic this time of night."

"Of course not. Who'd want to come into Loomis on a Sunday after dark?" She smiled, but she knew why he was here. Her expression was tight with it.

"Me. If I knew you were waiting for me here." He meant it, and the knowledge was a hard kernel of need in his gut. He had expected Jodie to be trouble. Because she was young. Because she was a rookie agent. Instead, she'd shown herself to be confident, mature beyond her years, able to do the job she had to do with single-minded determination. He admired that.

He admired her.

"You have a way with words, Cahill, but I'm sure you didn't come here to try and charm me."

"You're right." He stepped onto the porch, pulling Jodie close and looking into her face, knowing that what he had to say would change her forever. "There's no easy way to say this, Jodie."

"Easy isn't part of your job. I know that, Harrison." She brushed hair from her cheek, her hand trembling. "So, just say it."

"My friend called with the results of the DNA test. It was a match. Jane Doe is your mother."

She nodded and turned to stare into the dark night. "I've known it all along, but it's still hard to hear."

"I know. I'm sorry." He placed his hands on her shoulders, pulling her back against his chest and wrapping his arms around her, wishing he could do more. Offer more.

"When I was growing up, I imagined Mom off somewhere, creating a great life with a wonderful man," Jodie said distantly. "Someone who loved her and would love me. I really believed that one day she'd come and knock on the door and tell my father she wanted me to come live with her. It took me years to accept that she never would. Even then, I hoped that she'd come looking for me one day." She leaned against him then, her back warm against his chest, her hands resting on his forearms, the touch tentative and light. The flowery scent that seemed so much a part of who she was filled the air, filled Harrison's senses, making him want to pull her in closer, lean down and inhale the fragrance.

"She would have. I don't think she ever meant to leave you."

"No. I don't, either." Her words were so soft, he barely heard them. "I think that's the saddest part of it. That I spent years despising her for leaving me with a man who didn't love me when all along she never planned to go."

"How could you have known?" He shifted his grip, turning her around so they were face-to-face, his heart breaking when he saw the tears in her eyes.

"She was my mother. Shouldn't I have realized that she would never leave me?" Her voice broke, and a single tear slid down her cheek.

"Jodie—"

"It's okay. I'm okay." She brushed the tear away, and he knew she hated to cry. Hated to be vulnerable and weak.

"I know you are." He took her hand, tugging gently until she stepped into his embrace.

Her arms wrapped around him, and she lay her head against his chest, her breathing hitched, her body trembling.

"It's going to be okay." He smoothed her hair, letting his hand rest on the nape of her neck.

"I know." She sniffed, pulling away and wiping at her cheeks. "Thanks for coming to tell me, Harrison."

"What else would I have done?"

"Called. Waited until tomorrow when you actually planned to come back to Loomis."

"You know me better than that, Jodie. This isn't just a case to me. It's personal." He traced her jaw with his finger, lingering for a second at the corner of her mouth.

"It shouldn't be." She sighed, but didn't move away from his touch.

"Sometimes what we think should be is completely different than what God wants."

"Are you trying to say God wants you and me together?"

"I'm saying that there's something going on between us. We both feel it."

"Maybe we do, but that doesn't mean we have to act on it."

"It doesn't mean we shouldn't, either."

She rubbed a hand down her face and shook her head. "I've got to tell my father the news. Have you called the sheriff?"

She'd purposely changed the subject, but Harrison didn't mind. Now wasn't the time to talk about their relationship. They *would* talk about it, though. He was sure of that. "No. I wanted to talk to you first."

"Because you know my father is now the prime suspect in the murders."

"Until we know who the other victim is, yes."

"Go ahead and call him. I'm going inside to see how Dad takes the news." She paused with her hand on the doorknob. "If you want, you can come in after you make the call. Susan made apple cobbler. She's expecting you to have some."

"Sounds good, but only if you want me there." He put her on the spot, forcing her to issue the invitation. He wouldn't pursue a woman who didn't want a relationship. No matter how much he might want to.

She hesitated, her eyes dark and haunted. Finally, she nodded. "I do."

"Then tell Susan I'd love some apple cobbler." He watched her until the door closed, then pulled out his cell phone and dialed the sheriff's number.

It took less than twenty minutes for Sheriff Reed to arrive. Jodie heard his car pull into the driveway as she spooned up apple cobbler. She chewed by rote, the sweet dessert like cardboard in her mouth. Her father hadn't been a good parent. Actually, he'd been a pretty bad one, but that didn't mean she wanted him accused of murder, and it certainly didn't mean she wanted him to go to jail.

Typical of Richard, he hadn't had much to say when she'd told him the news about his ex-wife. Just that it didn't surprise him that Amelia was with another man when she'd died.

"That's the sheriff." Harrison's words broke the silence that had held the house in its grip since she'd taken her father aside and explained who had been found in the Underground Railroad room.

"I know."

"Does your dad know he's coming?"

"I told him to expect it, but he and Susan are holed up in his office, and I'm not sure whether he really believed he'd be a suspect in Mom's murder." Saying the words didn't hurt nearly as much as Jodie thought they would.

"He's going to believe it soon. Sheriff Reed sounded like he was ready to slap handcuffs on your father and cart him away."

Jodie's heart jumped at his words, sick dread filling her stomach. "He doesn't have enough evidence to do that."

"You're right. He doesn't. And you and I will make sure he knows it." Harrison hooked an arm around her waist and led her to the front door.

You and I. As if he planned to stay with her and face whatever trouble was coming.

Maybe he did.

He'd said there was something between them. Jodie couldn't deny it any more than she could deny the fear that filled her as she pulled open the front door and let the sheriff in. He wore civilian clothes, the faded jeans and soft plaid shirt making him seem almost approachable.

"Sheriff Reed. It's nice to see you."

"I'm sure you know why I'm here, Jodie. And I hope you're not going to try to stop me from doing what I have to."

"And exactly what is it you have to do, Bradford?" Richard walked out of his office, his strident voice echoing in the foyer.

"Maybe we should go in your office to discuss it."

"We'll discuss it here. There's nothing you have to say that my family can't hear."

"Have it your way, Richard." The sheriff shrugged, his jowly face nearly vibrating with irritation. "Here are the facts— twenty-five years ago your wife walked out on you. Disappeared, never to be heard from again."

"Wife? She filed divorce papers."

"And if I remember correctly, Amelia was rumored to have had a great lawyer. Seems to me, a man like you might not want to pay part of his salary to a woman who cheated on him, if that woman got a good divorce settlement. It's pretty convenient, her disappearing like that."

"What are you implying, Bradford?"

"I'm not *implying* anything. I'm stating it flat-out. You had more motive than anyone to kill Amelia Pershing Gilmore— your wife."

"Sheriff Reed—" Jodie tried to step in, but her father's hand slashed down, his face red with rage.

"I will handle this, Jodie. No one comes in my house and accuses me of murder."

"I'm not accusing you of anything. I'm asking. Did you follow Amelia to that old house by the bayou? Did you see her go in with her lover and decide that you could kill two birds with one stone…literally?"

"I did no such thing."

"Come on, Richard. A man like you couldn't have enjoyed being the butt of gossip and jokes. Your wife's betrayal had to have rankled. I'm a man. I understand how that kind of thing could put a person right over the edge of reason."

"I did not kill Amelia!" Richard shouted so loudly the windows seemed to shake with it.

"Richard, calm down." Susan placed a hand on his arm, but he seemed beyond hearing, his eyes blazing.

"No one walks in my house and accuses me of such a vile crime. No one!" He pointed a finger at the sheriff, and Jodie was afraid he might hit the man.

She started toward them, but Harrison put a hand on her arm, pulling her back and whispering in her ear. "Don't. Your dad won't appreciate it."

True. Her father liked to believe he ruled the roost, that everything within his home was within his control. Not this time. This time he had no control at all over what was about to happen.

"You better watch your tone with me, Richard. I can throw you in jail for disorderly conduct."

"Disorderly conduct? You come into *my home* and accuse me of murder, and *I'm* the one being disorderly? Let me tell you something, Reed, I could have killed Amelia a million times during our marriage. She was a stubborn, loudmouth who didn't know her place. I was glad to be rid of her. Glad!" He gasped, his hand pressing against his chest, his mouth working but no sound coming out.

"Dad!" Jodie ran forward, grabbing his shoulder as he toppled over.

She couldn't hold his weight, and it was Harrison who caught him, lowering him to the ground, gently brushing her hands away as he felt for a pulse.

"Someone call an ambulance." His voice was as calm as a frozen lake, his movements precise and measured as he leaned over Richard and began CPR.

"Dear Lord, please save him." Susan's soft cry echoed in Jodie's brain as she ran for the phone and dialed 911.

TWENTY-TWO

Jodie paced the waiting room of the hospital's cardiac unit, her legs leaden and heavy, her stomach churning. It had been seven hours since they'd brought her father in, stabilized but critical, three hours since they'd taken him in to do surgery on blocked arteries in his heart. She wanted to believe he'd survive the procedure, but she'd seen him lying on the floor, his lips blue, his body limp as they'd shocked his heart into beating again.

She shuddered, rubbing her arms and willing away the cold that had taken up residence in her heart.

"You need to sit down before you fall down." Harrison grabbed her hand as she passed his seat, pulling her down onto the chair beside him, his gaze so filled with compassion that Jodie's throat tightened and tears filled her eyes.

"I should have told him I loved him. One time in the past ten years, I should have said it."

"It's not too late." His palms brushed her cheeks, wiping away the tears.

"You don't know that."

"I do." He threaded a finger through her hair, urging her to rest her head against his shoulder, his solid strength making her yearn for what she'd never had. Support. Comfort. Love.

If she was ever going to have those things, it would be with someone like Harrison. Someone who understood loss, who had lived it, but who had learned to go on. "You're good for me. You know that, Cahill?"

"And you're good for me." His lips pressed against the top of her head, his arms tightening around her. She wanted to burrow closer, steal some of his heat, let it chase away the chill.

Instead, she backed away, putting a little space between them. "Dad has been in surgery a long time."

"No longer than the doctor expected."

"Longer than I expected, though." Jodie glanced at her stepmother, who'd fallen asleep in a chair. "At least Susan is getting some rest. Poor Susan. She really does love him."

"I think your father is a fortunate man to have a daughter like you and a wife like Susan." He stroked her hair, the smooth motion soothing Jodie as nothing else had.

"A daughter like me? This is the first time I've seen Dad in ten years."

"You gave your dad what he wanted—his freedom. That's the best you could offer him."

"Thank you for saying that."

"It's the truth. You know that, right?"

She looked into his eyes, saw the integrity that was so much a part of who he was. She saw something else, too. Something that promised more than she'd ever thought she'd have. "Harrison, I'm not sure I can give you what you want."

"What do you think I want?"

"A woman who can be everything to you."

"Then you've got nothing to worry about. All I want is you." He smiled, and Jodie's heart melted.

"Mrs. Gilmore?" A doctor stepped into the room, his expression somber, and Jodie jumped away from Harrison, reaching to grab Susan's hand.

"Susan?"

Her stepmother jerked awake, her gaze jumping to the doctor as she leaped from her seat. "What is it? Is Richard…"

"He's out of surgery and holding his own. We're hopeful he'll make a full recovery."

"But the heart attack…"

"Not as bad as it could have been. There's been some damage to the heart, but things could have been a lot worse."

"Can we see him?" Jodie stepped forward, knowing that Harrison was just a few inches behind her, his presence as comfortable and comforting as an old friend's.

"One at a time and just for a few minutes. We need him to rest so he can heal more quickly."

"Thank you, Doctor. Thank you." Susan was crying openly as she followed the doctor down the corridor, her soft sobs sounding through the quiet hospital.

"I told you it wasn't too late." Harrison dropped an arm across Jodie's shoulder and pulled her in to his side.

Exhausted, Jodie let him support her as she waited for Susan's return. It was only fifteen minutes, but felt like a lifetime before Susan reappeared, her pretty face haggard, her eyes shadowed.

"He's in room 406, and he's awake and talking, but loopy from the medicine. Thank the good Lord, he's okay. I told him you were here and would be coming in to visit. I'm going to call Reverend Harmon and ask him to inform the prayer loop that Richard has pulled through the surgery." She pulled out her cell phone and dialed, walking to the far side of the room and speaking quietly.

"You going to see him?" Harrison's arm dropped away, his gaze steady as he searched her face.

"Yes, but the sad thing is, I'm not even sure he'll want to see me. You said it yourself—all Dad really wants from me is his freedom."

"That's what he wanted, but maybe this has changed him."

"You don't think that, Cahill. Neither do I. But I'm going anyway. And I'm going to say exactly what I need to—that I love him."

"Good." Harrison smiled and ran a hand along his jaw. "Want me to call Sam and tell him you're not going to be in today?"

"I'll give him a ring after I'm done here." Because Richard might not want her around, and going to work might be better than staying where she wasn't wanted.

Her stomach churned as she stepped into her father's room. He seemed to have shrunk, his robust figure shrouded in sheets and tubes.

"Dad? Are you awake?" She almost hoped he wouldn't open his eyes, almost hoped that he wouldn't respond.

He did, his blue eyes peering out from his colorless face.

"I thought you were dead." The words rasped out, dry and cracked and old.

"No, I—"

"You coming to meet me and bring me to the other side with you, Amelia? I'm not coming. I've finally got something I always wanted. Someone who loves me for me."

"Dad. It's me, Jodie."

"Jodie. Selfish brat, that girl." He shook his head, closed his eyes.

"Dad?" Jodie tried again, taking his hand, trying not to be hurt by his words. He didn't know what he was saying. Didn't even know who he was talking to.

His eyes opened again, and he stared at her blankly, as if he were looking at a stranger.

"Dad, I know I haven't always been the greatest kid, but I want you to know something. I love you."

In a perfect world, he would have said he loved her, too. She would have leaned down and kissed his cheek, stroked his hair, told him he was going to be fine and that when he got out of the hospital they'd build the relationship they'd never had.

But Jodie didn't live in a perfect world, and her father said nothing, just closed his eyes, turned his head and drifted off to sleep.

"Miss? Your stepmother would like to come in again now. Are you finished?" A nurse appeared in the doorway, and Jodie stood, glancing at her father one more time before nodding at the nurse and walking out of the room.

Harrison was waiting for her at the end of the corridor, a five-o'clock shadow giving him a craggy, hardened look that didn't match the worry in his eyes. "How did it go?"

"Just like I expected."

"I'm sorry, Gilmore. I was hoping for more for you." He pulled her into his arms, holding her close, letting her feel the rhythm of his heartbeat.

"I'm okay."

"Are you?" He looked into her eyes, his fingers kneading the tight muscles in her neck.

"I don't have a choice. I've always taken what life has given me and gone on. I'll do the same this time."

"Only this time you don't have to go it alone." He leaned down, his lips brushing hers, the touch so gentle and light it was barely there, yet so powerful it shook Jodie to the core.

"Harrison—"

"My dear, I am so sorry to hear about your father's heart attack." A soft voice interrupted before Jodie finished.

That was good, because she wasn't sure what she would have said. That she wanted to believe Harrison? That she wanted to trust him? That she was more scared than she'd been in years, afraid that the things she saw in his eyes were simply a reflection of her own dying dreams.

She stepped away from his embrace, turning to face the woman who was coming toward them. Charla Renault, her hair perfectly coiffed despite the earliness of the hour, her electric wheelchair humming softly, a stunning redhead by her side.

"Mrs. Renault, it's so nice of you to come." Jodie schooled her features to hide her surprise. Her father had been married to a Pershing. The fact that the matriarch of the Renault family was at the hospital to visit him didn't make sense.

But, then, things often didn't make sense in Loomis.

"How could I not, when your father is here struggling for life. We were good friends years ago, Richard and I. Did you know that?"

"No, I didn't."

"I've never forgotten how kind and charming your father was. When Reverend Harmon called to ask for our prayers, I just knew I had to come and see him. As the reverend said at church, we must always be willing to forgive and move on." She smiled, but it didn't reach her eyes.

Jodie doubted she really planned to forgive or forget anything. "I'm sure my father will appreciate your visit."

"Yes, well, I'm just glad Ava agreed to bring me. I'm unable to drive since my accident, you know. You do remember my daughter?"

"I'm sure we saw each other when we were in high school." Jodie smiled at the woman who looked as uncomfortable as Jodie felt.

"I'm so sorry about your father, Jodie. I'll be praying for you." Ava sounded much more sincere than her mother, and she stepped forward to offer a quick hug. "How is he?"

"The doctor said he's holding his own. Susan is in with him now."

"Mother, maybe we should go home and come back when he's more rested."

"Of course we shouldn't. Richard will want to see me. Why don't you go find some coffee while I visit?"

"I—"

"Really, Ava, there is no sense in all of us standing around here."

"Of course. I'll be back in a few minutes." She offered a tight smile and a quick goodbye before walking away, and Jodie had the feeling her relationship with her mother was as strained as Jodie and her father's had always been.

"Mrs. Renault, if you'd rather go with your daughter—"

"Don't be silly, my dear. I'm fine here until your father can see me. Tell me, how have things been going since you arrived in town? There's been so much going on in Loomis. None of it very pleasant." Her gaze went from Jodie to Harrison and back again.

"We've been working hard to close our case." Jodie shifted uneasily, not comfortable with the direction of the conversation. She didn't want to discuss the Leah Farley case with Charla. She didn't want to discuss any of the cases with the woman. Like so many others, the Renault matriarch loved to gossip, spinning tales to suit her agendas. Whatever those might be.

"And have you found anything that might help you solve the crimes? Any evidence that might point to the criminal in our midst?"

"Mrs. Renault, that's not information that I'm at liberty to discuss." Weary, Jodie rubbed her forehead and wished she could find a graceful way to ask Charla to leave. She was too tired to go a round with the woman.

"Well, why not? I'm a taxpaying citizen. I have every right to know what is being done to keep my town safe." Charla sat up straight in the wheelchair, her eyes flashing.

"I understand, but many of the crimes aren't within the

FBI's jurisdiction. You'd be better off asking the sheriff for the information."

"I heard that there was blood on Leah's shoe that was found. Earl's blood." She shuddered, undaunted by Jodie's words.

"It wasn't Earl's blood, Mrs. Renault."

"No?" Her eyes widened. "Then whose?"

"We're not sure. DNA tests were inconclusive." Jodie didn't offer any more than that.

"Inconclusive? That's just not acceptable."

"But it's the information we have. The rest isn't something that Jodie is at liberty to discuss." Harrison cut into the conversation, his hand on Jodie's shoulder, his support unexpected and welcome.

"But surely you know something? People have been murdered. *My son* has been murdered. Do you even have a suspect?"

"We're not at liberty to say." Harrison's tone was calm, but his fingers tightened on Jodie's shoulder, and she knew he was irritated with Charla's pushiness.

"You found evidence. With forensic science being what it is, you must know something. I want answers, and I deserve them." Charla didn't raise her voice, but her anger was obvious, and Jodie suddenly understood why she was there. Not to visit the sickbed of an enemy's ex-husband but to pick Jodie's brain.

"Everyone deserves answers when a tragedy happens, but you'll have to bring your son's case up with Sheriff Reed."

"Young man, do you have children?"

"Not yet." He met Jodie's eyes and smiled.

Her heart jumped, her cheeks heated, but she didn't look away. Couldn't look away.

"Then you can't understand what it is like to lose a child. Unlike Jodie's mother, I loved my children beyond reason."

The blow was harsh and unexpected, and despite knowing what she did about her mother, Jodie reeled from it.

She took a step away from Harrison and Charla. "I'm sorry. I've got to leave. I need some air."

She didn't look at either again as she turned and ran from the waiting room.

TWENTY-THREE

It took Harrison less than a minute to say goodbye to Charla, another three to let Susan know that Jodie had left and would be back later and two more to listen as Susan assured him that she'd be fine until they returned.

By the time he reached the parking lot, Jodie's car was gone. Gray morning light glinted off his windshield as he hopped into his car and pulled out onto the road. He assumed Jodie would return to her father's house and went there, but Jodie's car wasn't in the driveway.

Concerned, Harrison glanced at the clock on his dashboard. It was just before seven. Too early for Sam to be at headquarters. Would Jodie have gone there?

He doubted it.

She would have wanted to be alone. To think. To nurse her wounds. To absorb everything that had happened. He considered leaving her alone, giving her the space and the time she needed to grieve. He couldn't. He realized now that he cared too much.

He grabbed his cell phone, dialing Sam's number, not caring if he woke the agent.

"Sam Pierce here."

"Sam, it's Harrison."

"Hey, I was just getting ready to call Jodie. My fiancée is

on the prayer chain at church and got a call saying Richard had a heart attack. She called to let me know."

"Yeah. It happened last night. Sheriff Reed was questioning him about Amelia Gilmore's murder."

"So it *was* Jodie's mother in that room."

"I'm afraid so."

"Tell her I'm sorry, and she should take as much time off as she needs."

"That's the thing, Jodie took off from the hospital, and I'm not sure where she went. I've got the phone number to her father's house, but not her cell phone. Do you have it?"

"Sure do. Hold on, let me look it up." A few seconds later, Sam rattled off the number, and Harrison scribbled it down. He tapped his fingers impatiently as Jodie's cell phone rang, and when she didn't pick up, he scowled. She could be halfway to New Orleans by now, but he doubted she'd go that far.

Frustrated, he pulled out of the Gilmore's driveway and onto the road, driving through town and then out of it, heading toward the bayou, instinct pulling him toward the place where Amelia had been found.

Jodie squeezed through the tunnel that led to the room where her mother's body had lain, her heart beating a hard, heavy rhythm. Twenty-five years ago, Amelia had come this same way, seen the same darkness beckoning her forward. Had she inhaled the musty air in the moments before she'd died? Had she known that death was coming for her?

Jodie shuddered, the beam of the flashlight she'd brought from her car dancing across the floor in front of her.

She shouldn't have left the hospital. Shouldn't have run out on Harrison and Susan. And she most certainly shouldn't be here. She didn't even know why she'd come. For closure? For answers? She wasn't sure she'd ever have either of those things.

Someone had killed her mother and the man she was with, but it hadn't been Richard. Jodie was certain of that.

Who then? And why?

Once they identified the male victim, they might find an answer. Until then, Jodie would just have to pray for peace.

She sighed, stepping into the room where her mother had died, listening to the silence and feeling the cool moist air press against her cheeks. A tomb that had finally released its dead. Empty now.

She aimed the beam of her flashlight toward the place where her mother had been found and swallowed back her tears. "I understand now, Mom. And I'm sorry."

Her words whispered on the air and faded away, gone as surely as Amelia Pershing Gilmore was.

A soft sound broke through the silence. Fabric brushing against the walls of the tunnel. The pad of shoes on dirt.

Jodie froze, the image of the figure she'd seen the previous day flashing through her mind. Alarmed, she flicked off her flashlight and moved to the far wall, waiting as the sounds grew louder, her hand reaching for her gun before she realized it wasn't there.

Tense, anxious, she peered into the darkness, stiffening as a beam of light appeared. Moments later a dark figure stepped into view. Not tall. Very slim. A woman? Maybe, but that wasn't enough to make Jodie relax. Women were just as capable of murder as men.

The beam of light drifted along the floor, following the same path Jodie had taken when she entered the room, lit on Jodie's feet and traveled up to her face.

"Jodie Gilmore. Why am I not surprised?"

"Mrs. Peel?" Jodie turned on her own flashlight, aiming the beam at the woman's face. "What are you doing here?"

"I could ask you the same, but I won't." Her cold eyes dropped to the floor, her lips twisted in what could almost pass as a smile. Almost.

"This is a crime scene, Mrs. Peel. You need to leave."

"Do I?" She looked around, that same strange smile on her face. "I don't see why. I've been visiting this place for years. Twenty-five years, to be exact. This is the first time since they died that I've been in this room, though. It's nice to finally come back."

Jodie went cold at her words, the sick, wild thudding of her heart nearly drowning out Vera's next words.

"Imagine my surprise when I came the other day and saw you here. And then to come so early and see you again. Well, it's just meant to be."

"What's meant to be?" Jodie sidled along the wall, moving out of the beam's light, knowing that she could take Vera down easily but wanting to get her story, to hear what she had to say.

"Your death, of course. Kind of like that poor Mary Sampson. Why she'd come to the bayou to take pictures on that day, I don't know, but when she saw me here…well, I knew it was meant to be. A sign from God. After all, what if she'd told someone I'd been here? You know how people in Loomis like to talk."

"Yes, I do."

"She was a kind woman. Really. So I didn't throw her in the bayou. I left her where she could be found. Her funeral was lovely." Her eyes glittered in the darkness, her lips still twisted in an evil smile. "Your mother. Now she was a different story. I trusted her, and she betrayed me. She stole my husband."

"Your husband?"

"Didn't they teach you anything in FBI training? Of course, my husband. Perceval said they fell in love. That Amelia was getting a divorce so they could be together. He wanted a divorce from me, too, but I refused. Marriage is for life, you know."

"Yes, I know."

"Well, I'm surprised you do. Your mother certainly didn't

have the same idea." She pulled something from her purse, and Jodie froze.

A gun.

The same weapon that had been used to kill Amelia and Perceval?

"Mrs. Peel, I know you've made some mistakes, but killing me will only make things worse."

"Mistakes? You're wrong, Jodie. If I'd made mistakes, I would have been caught, but I wasn't. And I won't be caught this time. God is on my side. All the evidence has already been collected from this room. It'll be another twenty-five years before someone comes in here and finds you." She lifted the gun, and Jodie dove to the side as the first bullet flew.

Her knees and elbows hit the ground and she rolled, dirt flying, Vera's rage-filled scream filling her ears.

Jodie came up, rushing low, ready to do whatever it took to survive. There was no way she was going to die in this little underground room. No way she'd lie abandoned for the next twenty-five years.

Please, Lord, don't let me die here.

"You *will* die like your mother. You will." Vera fired again, the shot skimming across Jodie's upper arm, warm blood spilling down to her elbow.

She didn't feel it. She was too focused on escaping. She came up fast, shoving into Vera.

The older woman fell back, then moved forward again, chanting under her breath, "Die. Die. Die."

No time to think about it. No time to be afraid.

Jodie lifted her flashlight, swinging it toward Vera's head, as a dark figure rushed from the tunnel and tackled the older woman to the ground.

Vera screamed, clawing and kicking. "Let me go. Let me go. I can't let her live. She stole my husband. She stole him from me."

"Sorry, lady, but I'm not letting you go until the police get here."

"Harrison?" Jodie flashed the beam of her light in his direction, sagging with relief when she saw his face.

"Who else? Are you okay?" He stood, pulling the now silent Vera to her feet.

"Fine."

"You're bleeding."

"Not much."

"Any is too much. I should have realized sooner that you'd be here."

"I'm just glad you realized it at all. You saved my life, Harrison." She reached down and lifted Vera's gun, pointing it at the older woman, who now seemed to have retreated into herself, her tall thin frame shriveled and empty-looking.

"You were managing just fine on your own, but I'm glad I could be here for you." He smiled, and Jodie felt all the fear, all the worry she'd been feeling, fade.

"I'm still going to call you my hero."

He chuckled, the sound echoing through the room. "We'll see if you still feel that way in a year or two."

"A year or two?" Her heart leaped at the words, all the things she'd thought she never have, suddenly within reach.

"Or fifty. Now, how about we escort Mrs. Peel upstairs and call the sheriff? The sooner she's behind bars, the happier I'll be." He hauled Vera toward the tunnel, and Jodie followed, turning one last time to look at the place where her mother had died, whispering words she knew Amelia would never hear. "Goodbye, Mom."

The sheriff arrived quickly, a posse of squad cars following him as if he were afraid the older woman he was taking into custody would fight him.

Jodie could have told him there was no fear of that. Vera

seemed almost catatonic, sitting on the front porch, staring into space as Harrison stood over her.

"What happened here?" Sheriff Reed spoke as he got out of his car, glancing at Jodie's blood-soaked sleeve and then at Vera.

"She confessed to killing my mother and Mary Sampson."

"Is this true, Vera?" Reed crouched in front of Vera, looking into her blank eyes.

She blinked, then seemed to focus on him. "Marriage is for life. I couldn't let Amelia break up something that was God-ordained. You understand, don't you?"

"Sure. Sure I do. And I hope you understand what I have to do." He read her Miranda rights, then gently pulled her to her feet, his compassion for the woman a stark contrast to the in-difference he'd seemed to have toward her victims.

"I just helped her into Heaven. That's all." Vera seemed to be speaking more to herself than to anyone else, but Jodie heard and shuddered, leaning into Harrison as he pulled her to his side.

"I'm sure you did, Vera. What'd you do, follow her here?" The sheriff took Vera's arm and led her away from the house, questioning her as they walked to his cruiser.

"Oh, no. I asked her to come to tea while my husband was at work and my daughter was at school. It was easy enough to hit her over the head, but then she was moaning and moving, and I wanted to make sure she was dead, so I shot her with Perceval's gun."

"And you brought her here later?"

"No, no. She was small, you know. And there was no one around. I just put her in my car and brought her here. I thought I would throw her in the bayou, but I wanted Perceval to see that there would be no future with her. I wanted him to know I was all he had. At first I just dragged her into the house, but then I was afraid someone would find her before I brought Perceval, so I ripped down the boards on the tunnel and dragged her inside."

"And then you went and got Perceval?"

"Oh, yes. He'd just gotten home from work. I told him we needed to talk somewhere where our child couldn't hear. I brought him down into the tunnel and showed him Amelia's body. He called me a murderer. He told me I would rot in jail. *He told me he would never stay with me.* Because of her!" She turned, breaking away from the sheriff's hold and turning to face Jodie. "You will die! You will!"

Jodie winced away from the harsh screams. Horrible images filling her head—her mother at tea with a friend, hit over the head, shot, dragged into the tunnel.

Jodie turned, running to her car, wanting to drive away and never look back.

"Jodie?" Harrison captured her hand, pulling her to a stop. Pulling her into his arms. "You don't have to run anymore."

Her breath caught at his words, her body stilling. Everything she wanted, everything she'd ever dreamed of was within reach.

If only she'd take it.

She took a deep breath, stared into his eyes for a long moment then wrapped her arms around his waist, tears of joy mixing with tears of sorrow as she stood on her toes and whispered in his ear. "I know."

EPILOGUE

Loomis, Louisiana
March 20, Vincetta's Italian Ristorante
7:00 p.m.

Jodie stepped into Vincetta's, her gaze scanning the tables as she searched for the only person she wanted to see. He was there, sitting in a booth near the window, his face turned toward the door. Waiting for her.

The knowledge filled Jodie with warmth, and she crossed the room, taking a seat next to Harrison, smiling into his eyes. "You waited for me."

"I'd wait a lifetime if I had to. Fortunately, it was only a half hour." He smoothed loose strands of hair away from her face and pressed a tender kiss to her lips.

"I'm sorry I couldn't get here on time. We were packing up headquarters and closing up the office. It took longer than I expected."

"But now you're here." He traced a line from her elbow to her wrist, stroking the tender flesh there. "And let me just say, you were well worth the wait."

"We'll see if you're still saying that in a year or two." She echoed the words he'd spoken in the tunnel, capturing his hand

and pressing her palm to his. Connected. Belonging as she never had before.

"A year or two?" He raised a brow, his eyes filled with amusement.

"Or fifty."

"Or more."

She laughed and shook her head. "Or more. Happy now?"

"Very." He sobered, scanning her face. "How about you?"

"I'm happy with you, and thankful that I have answers. That I know what happened to my mother. I just wish…"

"That none of this had happened?" He squeezed her hand, and she knew he'd always be there for her. Steady and sure. Offering her a place where she could be exactly who she was. Exactly the person God planned for her to be.

"No. I wish that my mother's last moments hadn't been so terrible. I wish that my father could love me the way other fathers love their daughters. But I won't wish these past few weeks away. If they hadn't, I wouldn't have met you."

"There is that." He smiled tenderly, pulling her close. "Did you finally tell your father what happened?"

"Yes. He seemed indifferent. Maybe he thinks my mother deserved what she got."

"No one deserves to be murdered."

"Vera sure thought people did. Poor Mary Sampson. She was simply in the wrong place at the wrong time. When the sheriff searched Vera's house, he found the gun used to kill Perceval and my mother hidden in a safe in Vera's attic room. There was a roll of film there, too. When the film was developed, there were photographs of Mary's husband and kids, of the bayou at sunset and of the abandoned house. Vera's car is clearly visible in one of them. The sheriff is speculating that with her husband out of town and her kids away, Mary decided to go for a hike. She lived two miles from the bayou. It isn't a stretch to think she grabbed her camera and went out to shoot photos."

"So, Vera killed her there and transported her to the gazebo."

"That's what she admitted to, but we know Mary was alive when she was transported. Vera realized it when she got to the gazebo and hit her again before leaving her to die."

"Did Reed find the weapon?"

"No, and Vera is too far gone to give much more information. Chuck was at Vera's house when the sheriff arrived. He had to be forcibly removed from his room. He's still insisting someone is going to kill him."

"Maybe he knows about Vera's crimes."

"Or maybe he knows about someone else's. Either way, he's terrified. Fortunately for him, Vera's daughter is willing to let him stay at the house for a while longer. Otherwise he'd be out on the street."

"I feel sorry for Vera's daughter. It can't be easy to learn that your mother murdered your father and his lover."

"Me, too. For a town that is so obsessed with motherhood, Loomis doesn't produce very good ones." Jodie sighed. "I know one thing for sure, I'm glad to be going home. With the DNA tests on Leah Farley's shoe coming back inconclusive, her trail has gone cold, so working from New Orleans makes more sense than staying here."

"And having us both working in the same city will make it a lot easier to plan our wedding."

"Wedding?" Surprised, Jodie backed away. "We've only known each other a few weeks. We can't plan a wedding."

"Maybe not now, but eventually. And when we do, living close to each other will make it easier."

"Harrison—"

"What?" He grinned, and Jodie knew she would never run again. Not from her dreams. And not from Harrison Cahill.

"You're right."

"I was hoping you would say that." He captured her lips with his, kissing her with passion and with promise. Everything Jodie had ever wanted was there in his arms.

"Sir? Ma'am? Are you ready to order?" The voice of the waitress was like a splash of ice water in the face, and Jodie jumped away from Harrison, blushing as she met the server's eyes.

"I think we need another minute."

"Of course." The young woman smiled and walked away, probably heading off to gossip about the FBI agent and the forensic anthropologist.

"I guess I've just put a black mark on your reputation." Harrison pulled her from her thoughts, and Jodie shook her head.

"It already has too many to count. Besides, I've realized that what people think of me is not nearly as important as what God thinks." She paused, movement outside the restaurant window catching her attention. A man had paused in front of Vincetta's and was staring at the sign, his expression unreadable. Hair a little too long. Face scruffy, with a five-o'clock shadow. A duffel bag in one hand. He looked menacing and somehow familiar.

"What is it?" Harrison glanced out the window, frowning as he caught sight of the man. "That guy looks like trouble."

The words brought back a memory. A younger version of the man. Scowling at teachers. Staring down bullies. Tough. Hard. Not someone to be messed with. Most of the older women in town had said he looked like trouble. Patrick Rivers. The name came to her along with a shiver of unease. "He did when he lived here, too."

"He's a local?"

"Was. He left Loomis the year before I did. There was some kind of scandal, and he was chased out of town."

"I wonder why he's back."

"Revenge? He wasn't treated well. It could be he wants Loomis to pay for that."

"Could be, Gilmore, but it's not our case to solve."

"You're right." She forced herself to turn away from window, to let go of the ideas that were racing through her mind. "How about we order?"

"I've got a better idea."

"What's that?"

"How about we go to your dad's and beg Susan for a meal? Then you can pack up your car and we can head back to New Orleans tonight. The sooner we get out of this town, the better."

"I—"

"I know for a fact Susan made some more of her apple cobbler."

"You spoke with Susan?"

"Sure did. I wanted to make sure she knew that we'd be back in the fall."

"The fall?"

"Remember that wedding I said we should plan?" He stood and pulled her to her feet. "I was thinking autumn would be the perfect time to have it. What do you think?"

What did she think?

She thought it sounded perfect. "I think that autumn is my favorite time of year."

Harrison laughed, putting an arm around her shoulders as they walked out of the restaurant.

The air was humid and tinged with the scent of the bayou. Despite her joy, Jodie shuddered. She was leaving Loomis, but in the months to come, she would continue to search for answers to Leah Farley's disappearance. She'd visit the little town that hid so many secrets, and she'd pray that, unlike Jodie's mother, Leah Farley would be found alive.

"You okay?" Harrison squeezed her shoulders, and she smiled.

"How could I not be when I'm with you?"

He laughed again, leaning down to kiss her before they walked to her car together, the scent of the bayou swirling around them, hinting at secrets and decay and a darkness that still stained the rich Loomis soil.

* * * * *

*Keep reading for a sneak preview of the
next exciting* **WITHOUT A TRACE** *book,
A CLOUD OF SUSPICION by Patricia Davids,
on sale in April.*

Dear Reader,

There have been times in my life when I've felt burdened by my mistakes. The weight of wrong decisions has dragged me down, and I have felt enslaved by my past. As a Christian, I have been able to go before Christ, lay my burdens at His feet and allow His peace to fill the hollow ache of regret. In *Cold Case Murder*, Jodie has many regrets. Her past is filled with small acts of rebellion. She feels tainted by her mother's sins, by her father's abuse and by the town she grew up in. She's spent years running from those feelings and from the past she hates so much. When she is forced to return to Loomis to help search for Leah Farley, she must face all the things she fears, and she must learn that God accepts who she is, where she is.

I hope you enjoy reading the third book in the WITHOUT A TRACE continuity as much as I enjoyed writing it. I love to hear from readers. You can contact me via e-mail at shirlee@shirleemccoy.com.

Blessings!

Shirlee McCoy

QUESTIONS FOR DISCUSSION

1. Jodie Gilmore left Loomis to escape. What was she running from? Has she managed to really leave those things behind?

2. Despite so many years away from the small town where she grew up, returning fills Jodie with the same feelings she had when she left. Why is it so hard for her to return as the accomplished professional she is?

3. Jodie believes in God, but she has no relationship with Him. What has kept her from pursuing a deeper understanding of Him?

4. Harrison Cahill has reasons for not wanting to be in a relationship with Jodie. What are they?

5. What eventually convinces him that Jodie is the right woman for him?

6. Harrison made decisions about his career based on his past. How does this enable him to better understand what drives Jodie?

7. Like Jodie, Vera Peel has lived her life in the shadow of the past. What mindset led her to act in the way she did?

8. How is it possible that someone who professes to be a Christian and understand Scripture can commit a truly horrible act?

9. Jodie's relationship with her father is difficult, but she finds a kindred spirit in Susan. What is it that brings the two together and helps them connect?

10. Harrison is open to God's plans for his life, but often works hard to make his own plans work out. At times, he is forced to step back and reevaluate the direction he's going in. Is it possible to seek God's will while pursuing our own desires and dreams? How can we know that what we want is also what God wants for us?

11. Loomis is a town steeped in bitterness. The people there suffer the consequences of a long-ago feud and two families' inability to forgive. Have there been times in your life when relationships with the people around you are strained by past arguments and disappointments?

12. What is God's command regarding forgiveness? How would life in Loomis be different if the people there lived in a way that honored God's command about it?

"It's been nearly three months since Leah vanished. How can the FBI still be clueless? What's the matter with you people?" Wendy Goodwin demanded.

"Hush, Wendy." Shelby Mason grabbed her cousin's arm. Throwing an apologetic look at the FBI agent Jodie Gilmore, Shelby asked, "Nothing new at all? I thought when I saw you back in town there might be a new lead."

Jodie's eyes held sympathy and understanding. "I'm only here because the home office received a phone tip we thought was worth checking into. It didn't pan out. We haven't had a solid new lead since the discovery of Leah's shoe in February at that abandoned house in the swamp."

The slipper hadn't led them to Leah. Instead, it had led investigators to uncover and solve a twenty-five-year-old triple murder. One of the victims had been Jodie's mother. Another Loomis woman who had vanished without a trace.

If anyone in the bureau would keep looking for answers, it would be Jodie.

Shelby nodded her thanks. She came by the sheriff's office at least three times a week to check in on her friend's case. As the months passed with no new information, the FBI's Missing Persons task force had gone back to New Orleans.

When Shelby saw Jodie today, her hopes had shot up, but once again she faced bitter disappointment.

Soon they would call off the search and give Leah up for dead.

"I think it's just criminal you people aren't doing more." Wendy raised her voice in a parting shot.

Shelby dragged her cousin out the door. Her sentiments might be the same as Wendy's, but she could never voice them the way her outspoken cousin did.

Once outside the sheriff's office, Shelby released Wendy. "I want Leah to be found as much as you do, but insulting the people looking for her isn't going to help."

Wendy crossed her arms and shivered, although the morning was warm with late-March sunshine and rising humidity. "It's just so frightening. How does someone we know vanish? This kind of thing only happens in movies."

"It happens in real life, too, Wendy."

"It doesn't happen to your friend. To someone who attends the same church. To someone who brings her daughter to our library for Story Hour."

Shelby drew Wendy close in a comforting hug. "I know. I'm frustrated, too, but the sheriff's office insists they are doing all they can."

"Do you think she's dead?" Wendy whispered.

Pulling back, Shelby gazed into her cousin's worry-filled blue eyes. With one hand she smoothed back a lock of Wendy's blond hair. "I can't think that way. I have to believe she's alive."

Please, Lord, let it be true for little Sarah's sake.

Wendy bit her lip. "After the other murders, it's hard to hold on to hope."

"That's why we have to put our faith in God. He's watching over Leah.

Wendy cast a glance around. "I know you're right, but you can't deny this is a scary time. I get up a dozen times at night to make sure the doors and windows are locked. I don't go out after dark. I don't let the kids play outside alone. I look twice at everyone I know and I think, could it be them?"

Depression dragged at Shelby's spirits. "I know. I feel the same way."

"The whole town is on edge. Some people are still insisting that Vera Peel is the serial killer. Dylan Renault and Angelina Loring were both struck over the head and shot in the back, just like the pair of skeletons that were found at that old house."

"Vera Peel confessed to killing her husband, Jodie's mother and that poor woman in the gazebo twenty-five years ago, but she has an alibi for the time of Dylan's murder. Besides, Leah's husband wasn't shot in the back."

"But Earl was shot. Some people are saying—"

"I know they're saying Leah killed Earl for the insurance money, that she panicked and skipped town, that she ran off with some unknown lover. None of it is true."

None of it makes sense. Lord, we need your help. Please keep Leah safe and bring her home to us.

Releasing her cousin, Shelby started toward the crosswalk at the corner of Church Street and Main. Their destination was the restaurant inside Loomis Hotel. Coffee made with chicory and scalded milk and the mouthwatering beignets at the posh Café au Lait were a Monday-morning custom the women had enjoyed for the past two years.

Shelby, Wendy and Leah had first chosen the high-class setting to celebrate Shelby's appointment as head librarian at the Loomis Public Library. The women had been starting their workweek in the same way ever since.

When Shelby and Leah's high-school friend, Jocelyn Gold, returned to Loomis to open a practice as a child psychologist, they were quick to include her in their tradition. They'd shared some great times and plenty of laughter together.

Knowing Leah wouldn't be joining them put a damper on what used to be a lighthearted gathering, but sticking to the ritual had become a means of keeping each other's sprits up.

"How can y'all be so sure Leah isn't guilty?" Wendy asked. "We never know what another person is capable of doing."

Shelby didn't hesitate. "Leah wouldn't abandon Sarah. That little girl is everything to her."

"You're right. I'm going crazy with all the uncertainty. Leah couldn't ask for a better friend then you, Shelby."

"I wish that were true. If I'd been a better friend, she might have confided in me. I knew something was bothering her, I just didn't thing it was any of my business."

They were almost at their destination when Shelby noticed a motorcycle occupying a parking space in front of the hotel. The custom chrome-and-black machine crouched in the line of sedans and SUVs, looking like a panther among a herd of milk cows.

The leather-studded saddlebags over the rear tire conjured up images of life on the road, escape, excitement, daring. All the things Shelby read about in the books at the city library where she worked, but had never experienced for herself.

Looking over her shoulder as she pulled open the café door, she couldn't help the wistful tone in her voice as she stepped inside. "I wonder who that belongs to."

"It's mine."

At the sound of a man's low, rumbling voice, electricity raced over her nerve endings. Her head whipped around, and Shelby found herself staring at the zipper of a black leather jacket decorated with the same silver studs as the saddlebags.

Looking higher, she met the owner's dark, hooded gaze, and recognition hit her like a kick to the stomach.

Patrick Rivers was back in Loomis.